For my grandfather, whom I never met, but also never jaundiced. May he rest in peace.

A Way Home

Meg Sechrest

Published by Meg Sechrest Books, 2018.

A WAY HOME

First edition. December 12, 2018.

ISBN: 979-8215867600

Written by Meg Sechrest.

One

The train ride home was always too long, or so it felt. Returning to the small town from the city each year for the holidays was becoming more of a task now that my parents were aging and my siblings found it impossible to come to a common ground on anything. Since my grandmother's passing, my siblings and I became responsible for the 1000-acre dilapidated farm. Passed down to us from my parents when they were no longer able to care for it, the burden now rested on us. The problem was that none of us lived there anymore, nor did we want the issue or headache of the maintenance of the farm. But written in small print was that it had to be sold in its entirety, which was nearly impossible with a farm of that size in that area. We were stuck with it.

So, every holiday, weekend off, or every other chance I could get, I took the train from Chicago to that small town in Colorado and checked in on my parents and the house that I co-owned with my four brothers. Nothing ever changed here, or so it seemed. The same old brick buildings with their simple, outdated business signs and the blinking yellow stop lights without a single crosswalk in the entire town made for a simple life. The people here were as simple as the town, if not more than, with their slowed speech and their improper clothing. Farm life was the way of life here; boots and hats, camouflage, and jeans were an everyday occurrence for most people in this town. It was perfectly normal to walk into the local diner or bar dressed in your farm best. I walked off that train, took a deep breath, looked around myself, tucked my scarf into my jacket, and walked down the stairs, preparing myself for a long holiday break.

"58647 North Country Road," I said to the cab driver at the train station.

"Is that Grove Station? The old Crashaw place?" he asked.

"Yes."

"Sorry, but that's a 45-minute drive from here. My route doesn't go that far."

Frustrated and tossing my hands into the air, I huffed, "Well what are you expecting me to do now?"

Thinking for a moment, he replied, "I'll be right back." Then he exited the car and walked away and into the local bar just a few hundred feet away. "Typical," I thought. Remembering why I left this area at 17 years old, I opened the back door and stood against the side of the cab, impatiently waiting for the driver to return. After a few minutes of petulantly tapping my foot against the sidewalk, he returned. "Ma'am? This is Michael Radcliff. Your name?"

"I'm just looking for a ride. I just need a way home," I said.

Michael looked at me somewhat confused and replied, "You live out at the big farm?"

"No. Technically, I don't live there. My parents do. I'm just here for the holidays. I'm a medical fellow in Chicago."

"Well, it's nice to meet you," he said extending his hand. "I'm heading out that way to take care of some things for your parents. I'd be happy to give you a lift." He started walking away to an old, beat-up pickup truck.

"Perfect," I replied, climbing in.

The cab driver tossed my bags into the back, gave the signal to Michael that all was good to go, and then we were off. We drove in silence at first and it was awkward, but I'll admit that I found this back-woods man somewhat attractive— even in all his roughness— though not in the usual sense that I would've been attracted to the city men; nonetheless, I looked at him and thought him handsome enough. He was dressed in a blue flannel shirt, which accented his bright blue eyes and blond hair that was wavy and messy from the day's work and was causing me to wonder what he did for a regular job, beyond the side job he was doing for my parents. I wanted to ask, but I didn't know if it would make things even more awkward than it already was.

As we stopped at a red light in a small town a little while later, I glanced in his direction for a quick moment and saw him looking out the side window at a big blue house, which struck my curiosity.

"Is that your house? Do you live there? It's beautiful," I asked.

"No." ... was all he said.

"Oh. Okay... I'm Hadley by the way."

"Thanks for the introduction, Hadley."

"You must've talked to one of my brothers," I mentioned.

"Excuse me?" he answered.

"When you set up maintaining the farm, it wasn't me."

"Obviously. I know the difference between men and women," he said.

"Right." Feeling embarrassed, I turned to look out the window, realizing he wasn't interested in conversation, and stayed quiet.

After a few moments, he moved his eyes in my direction and said, "So what brings you to town?"

"The usual. You know, arguing with my brothers... family things."

"I understand that."

"We are trying to sell the farm but we can't because there's some kind of legal issue with the deed."

Mentioning the deed perked his interest just a bit and he asked, "Oh? How so?"

"I'm not sure about the particulars. I just know that it has to be sold in its entirety, but we want to sell it in plots. I'm sure you don't want to hear about our family problems. Let's talk about something else."

"Of course. So, you're studying medicine. Anything specific?"

"I was just going for general practice, but after I completed my field of study, my grandma died from cancer..."

"So now you're in oncology," he finished.

"Yes."

He gave a sort of half-smile at my response, which brought my sassiness out, wondering what his smirk was about.

"What are you smiling about? Did I say something humorous with the word 'Yes'?"

Looking over at me a little flabbergasted at my smart mouth, he only said, "Just smiling at the irony."

"The irony of what? I'm sitting over here in the dark of your one-sided smirking irony."

He chuckled slightly, shaking his head, then he said, "Wow, you are nothing like the elder Crashaws, must be that city living." He said nothing else and no longer turned to look in my direction until we arrived.

"I don't pull up the drive to the house so as not to disturb your parents. You'll have to walk up the lane," he said and pointed up the long gravel drive to my parents' house. As I moved to exit he said, "I'll be in the barns and field most of the evening, if you need anything."

"Thank you for the ride. Have a good evening," I said, closing the door and walking away, wondering the mystery behind this handsome yet rough-looking man.

"Hi, Mama," I said walking into the house, but she didn't respond.

The movement I could hear in the kitchen I was certain was my mother as I listened to the banging of the pots and pans, and the slightly off-key humming of show tunes. "Mama?" I said once more, glancing around the kitchen door, to see her standing at the stove wearing her old patchworked apron and her long gray hair pinned up, stirring a pot of what I figured to be boiling potatoes.

"Mama," I said, walking over, taking the spoon from her hand, causing her to look up at me and wipe her hands on that tattered apron.

"Hadley? I didn't expect you so soon. What are ya doin' back so soon, baby girl?"

"Jackson called. He said there was a problem going on with Ethan and John."

She picked up the pot, walked over to the sink, covered it with the lid, and drained the water before saying, "Did you change your hair? It looks lighter now and shorter. I don't remember it being this blonde color and laying all the way up here on your shoulders how it is…"

"Mama, I'm here for a reason," I said, trying to get her focus off of me and back to why I came before Christmas.

"I know that Jack wants the sale deed on the farm changed so you all can sell it and be rid of it forever, but that's just not possible. You kids are fighting like cats and dogs over this mess and I wish you all could all just get along now. It's paining your father to watch all of this happen." Then she walked over to the stove once more and resumed mashing the potatoes. "Hady, hand me the milk and butter from the fridge, baby. I've got supper to get on the table. Oh, and be a doll and tell Michael out in the barn that we are having beef and potatoes tonight."

"What?"

"That farmhand your father hired…"

"Daddy hired him?"

"Of course. You didn't surely think we could manage all this on our own, did you now? Now go along and tell him that it's almost time to eat."

"He eats with you?"

"Well, certainly. You don't think I would let him stay out there in the cold and not offer him something to eat? What kind of person do you think I am? He doesn't have any family. He's such a handsome young man but has no wife or children of his own."

"What about that blue house in town?" I asked as I walked to the back porch door.

"What's that now?"

"When he was driving me out here, he stopped in Jenkins Hollow and was staring at a big, old blue house. What's the story about it?" I asked.

"I don't know anything about the blue house. He's a very private person and hasn't opened up much to us. We try talking to him when he comes in to eat, but he answers in mostly yes or no responses, and then he washes his own plate and heads back out to finish his work until dark."

As she was speaking, I glanced out the back-door window and watched him as he pulled the big, red tractor out of the barn and into the back field. My smile curled up just slightly while I watched and I wasn't even sure why. But I was feeling attracted to this man and felt I wanted to crack open his mysterious shell. Out the back door, I went.

"Michael!" I hollered, waving my arms, trying my best to get his attention.

When yelling and waving didn't do the trick, I hoofed it in my bare feet across the backyard all the way to the field where he was hauling hay for the horses.

"Michael!" I yelled, hands to my mouth to make a megaphone to carry my voice just a bit farther. "My mama wants you in for..."

"I'm not comin' in this evening!" he hollered back with a wave and a salute to his forehead. Then he resumed his driving.

I shrugged and turned around, walking back across the yard to deliver the message.

"Michael says he's not joining us this evening," I told her as I walked inside and saw her setting the kitchen table.

"What? Why would he go and say a thing like that?" she asked, turning to face me, placing the plates down, and removing her apron.

"Beats me," I said as I grabbed some silverware from the drawer to assist with setting the table. "He looked pretty immersed in working. Perhaps he just didn't want to be interrupted?"

"Pish posh! He always joins us! Did you open your sassy mouth and say something rude to him?" she asked, hands on her hips, almost scolding me.

"No! Why is this my fault? I've only met the man one hour ago."

"Well, never has he missed a supper is all," she said, turning to pick up the plates and place them across the table.

"I can assure you, Mama, this has nothing to do with me."

Joining the commotion just then as Daddy walked into the kitchen, planting a kiss on her cheek, he asked,

"What's all this about now? Hadley! When did you arrive? What are you doing here so soon?"

He walked over then to hug me and plant a kiss on my cheek too. Looking at my father, no one could tell I was his daughter. He was raised a farm boy and had the stature to show for it— tall, broad-shouldered, and even in his older age, he was still the picture of masculinity. His dark hair was graying now, but his brown eyes kept him looking young.

My mother, on the other hand, was petite—like me. Raised a city girl, she moved to the country with him when they were married and became a helper on his parents' farm only because she loved him not because it was her choice. Her lighter hair which wasn't brown but not quite blonde was graying and was usually kept pinned up and away from her face, and her blue eyes were always happy and sparkling. She was the image of beauty. I felt so at least. Did I look like my mother? In theory, yes. Did I have her beauty? Not exactly.

"I got in just a little while ago, Daddy. Michael brought me in from the train station. Apparently, he's the only taxi service that comes all the way out here these days."

"Oh! So, you've met our new farmhand! He's a great worker. We're hoping to keep him for a long time."

"I'm glad you have someone you like, Daddy. What happened to the last guy? Uh... Hank whatever?"

"Well, he turned out to be a thief!" Mama exclaimed. "He wasn't showing up on time and was skipping days for work. Then he started stealing your Daddy's tools."

"But you're not telling the entire story now, Mrs. Crashaw," Michael said, walking in through the back door, hanging up his coat on the hook beside the door, and kicking off his boots.

"What's the entire story?" I asked, watching him walk over as he ran his dirty fingers through his hair and shook himself off before washing his hands in the kitchen sink. And I admired his tall, muscular physique and the way he almost owned the room the moment he walked in without needing to demand it. It was like the way he moved and spoke commanded it of everyone.

"I won't be joining this evening. I just needed to wash off my hands. Work's all finished for today. There wasn't a lot to do. I'll be heading out now."

"What's the entire story?" I asked again.

"A hero came along and saved the day," he said.

He turned to exit just as my daddy said, "Let us repay you some other way then."

"No, thank you. You all have a good evening." Then he looked at me and said. "Glad I was there to help you out. Good evening, Ma'am." He slipped his boots back on and grabbed his jacket as he walked back out the door.

Wanting to know more, I hurried out the door behind him and ran barefoot down the gravel drive as he slowly walked to his truck.

"Michael," I breathlessly hollered, as he continued on. Determined to be my usual nosy self, I hollered out again. "What did you mean? What was all that about?"

He stopped immediately where he stood, and turning to face me, he said, "I saw an older couple in need of a kind gesture, so I did exactly what I felt should be done: I helped. I'm continuing to help because that's what life is all about— kindness and doing good with the little time we have on this earth. Now, if you don't mind, I've had a long day and I'd like to go home and take a shower."

"Yes, of course," I replied and watched intently as he walked the rest of the way down the long gravel drive to climb into his truck and leave the farm.

Once he was out of sight, I walked back up to the house and into the kitchen, sitting down at the table with my parents.

"Mama, tell me about how Michael started working here."

"Well, the last hand was stealing tools from us and your father was putting up posters up about him all over town. That's when Michael showed up at our door. He asked us about the man and knew right away who we were talking about..."

"But Michael said Daddy called him."

"I'm not finished," she corrected me, then continued, "Once he found the perpetrator, he returned our stolen tools and explained that this man had been known in nearby towns for doing this before..."

"How did Michael know this?" I asked, disbelieving.

"He has been working farms for many years. His father was a farmer and so was his grandfather..."

"I get it."

"Well, he left us his number in case we ever needed assistance again. But your father called him last spring when the ice started melting because some of the power lines to the cooling units in the dairy barns got pulled loose and your father couldn't fix them. So, Michael came over and broke the ice-free, thank goodness! After that day, he just started coming by every day to check on us. We didn't even have to ask. Your father offered to pay him, but he refused. When he saw us having supper one night, I asked him to join, but I think he felt awkward so I told him that's how I wanted to repay him for all his good service to us."

"Oh. He sounds like a very generous person. I wonder why he didn't want to stay this evening?"

"Too tired is all I can figure. Why don't you run on up and get yourself a bath and get cleaned up? Your father still watches game shows every evening."

When she said that, I realized that my luggage was still in the back of Michael's truck, and I had no way of contacting him or getting it back until he arrived tomorrow evening.

Two

After leaving the farm that evening, I needed to clear my head. Her full lips and beautiful eyes were clouding my mind and I could think on them no longer. Driving to the last place I needed to be, I settled in for a few hours to get her out of my thoughts.

"Are you sure?" Dina asked me as I walked in and took a seat at the bar.

"Yep."

"I know what this is," she said, turning around to get her bourbon, which had been my drink of choice these days.

"What is this?" I asked, downing my first shot.

"This is about that pretty Crashaw girl everyone is talking about. People been sayin' you drove her all the way out to her parent's farm this afternoon and that she's quite the looker with some of that fancy city charm you seem to like from your college days."

"So?"

"I know you, Michael Radcliff," she said, pointing to me as she turned her back to pour me another shot. "You want her and you want her bad. She ain't like all these simple country girls around here. She's different and it's caught your eye. You always liked different. Why'd you think you went out with me?"

"Dina, first of all, you think you know me because we used to date for like a week, but then you chucked me when I was too much man for you," I said, rolling my eyes, downing another shot. "Second, I went out with you because you were so damn persistent and you're not an ugly girl." At one time, she'd been a short-lived fancy of mine.

But that didn't remove the reality that she was correct; I did find Hadley especially attractive, though not in the usual sense that I looked at women. There seemed to be a certain innocence about Hadley Crashaw—which was incredibly appealing—and though I definitely wasn't looking for a relationship, I looked at Hadley and saw something in her form and personality that was drawing me to her and driving me crazy.

"I'm not ugly? Jeez, Mike. Thanks for the flattering compliment." She rolled her eyes.

"Mikey?!" my friend Billy hollered from the booth behind me.

"Maybe I don't know everything about you Michael Anthony Radcliff, but I know that you shouldn't be here."

"What's been going on with you? I haven't seen you in forever!" Billy said taking a seat on the barstool next to me, interrupting Dina's relentless meddling.

"He's been hanging out up at the old Crashaw place," Dina said.

"You mean John Crashaw's old farm?" he asked.

"Who?" I asked.

"You know who... John. We went to high school with him. He's got the three younger brothers that were always playing football and baseball, and a smokin' hot younger sister but she was a lot younger than us and was very nerdy back then."

"Oh, yeah. He knows the sister, alright. But I bet you wouldn't be finding her so nerdy now," Dina winked before she refilled both our glasses.

"What the hell is she yakking about?" he asked.

"Well, word around here is that she's still smokin' hot but now she's quite the catch," Dina said.

"Dina, aren't there other customers for you to wait on? Move along," I said with a wave of my hand.

She turned her nose up and walked to the other end of the bar.

"So, this sister... she's pretty hot?" he asked.

I glanced in his direction without saying anything, but I'm pretty certain my facial expression gave me away because he said, "What is it about her? What do you like? Give me an image. It's been a while for me and I just need to think about any girl other than Dina..."

Laughing at his reference to Dina, I replied, "She's not really your type. In fact, I don't even know what about her caught my attention. She's a blonde..."

"I like blondes."

"Forget it."

"Why? You think you automatically get her?" he asked, as I stood to leave.

"You know what? I think I'm good for tonight. Thanks, Dina." I left $30 on the bar for my shots and then I left.

But he hollered to the door behind me, "Consider this every man for himself when we live in towns as small as we do!"

Shaking my head and walking down the sidewalk, I decided I needed to take a long walk. However, my walks always ended in the same place— the big blue house.

"Michael?" Terry answered, "She's not here."

"I'm not here to see her. I just want to get a few of my things," I said, stepping inside.

"Alright." He moved aside and said, "You look like hell."

"I feel like hell. Thanks for the reminder."

When I took a look around, I felt angry at the entire situation and I just walked into the side room with the circle window and I rooted through the desk that was in there until I found some papers I wanted.

After the conversation I'd had with Hadley on the way to their farm earlier, I wanted to be sure I had some of the important documents and some of my books from my shelf that had been left there.

"Michael?! What are you doing here?!"

"I'm not here to cause trouble. I'm just on my way out," I said, looking at a woman I'd buried deep in my past.

"What did you take?" she asked.

"You know, this is my house. These are my things," I said.

"Fine. Take them. But don't come back."

"Keep talking to him that way, Janine and he'll kick your ass out on the street!" Terry hollered as I slammed the front door closed.

When I arrived home, a friend of mine was sitting on my front porch stairs waiting to greet me.

"Dina called," he said, standing, as I approached.

"Luke, you don't need to be here. I'm fine."

"Lie. Breathe on me," he said.

"I refuse," I said, unlocking the door to my rundown house, and walking inside.

Luke was my best friend and had been for a long time. In all my rough times when I had not a family member to call, he was there. He was the picture of redneck though—

boots, jeans, flannels and tees, messy brown hair, and a scruffy beard— but to me, he was my better half.

"She said you had a few shots," he accused, following me inside.

"Yeah, so what?" I asked, setting my things down in the kitchen, and then playing my phone messages.

You have 17 new messages...

"Hi. Michael, it's Shelley from the bank..."

I deleted that one and moved on.

"Michael, please call me back. I know you're probably wondering how I got this number but..."

Again, I deleted a familiar voice of my past and moved on.

"Michael, it's Dr. Ramirez..."

Noting that there were no messages I cared to hear, I went about my other business, moving beyond the machine.

"Mike, my friend, talk to me. What's going on?" Luke asked.

"Nothing is going on. If you're going to stand there, why don't you be of use and bring in the mail?" I said.

He sighed and turned to walk out and get the mail, letting the screened door slam shut on his way out.

As he was gone, I took the time to kick off my work boots and get a beer from the fridge, also looking for something to eat, now wishing I had taken dinner from Mrs. Crashaw. But the thought of her daughter was enough for any man to resist.

"Hey man, did you know you have some suitcases in the back of..."

"Shit!" I said, sitting down on my couch as Luke walked back in.

"I take it those aren't supposed to be there?"

"No. Do I travel?" I asked.

He shrugged.

"Whose are they?"

"I gave someone a ride today..."

"You mean a woman," he said, pointing to me as he turned slightly to face me and leaned down to get a beer from the fridge.

"Yes. It was a woman."

Sitting down next to me with a sly smirk, he asked, "Was she hot?"

I looked at him, somewhat irritated and not wanting to answer that, but he forced it.

"I know by your lack of response that she is. I know you, man. If she was hideous you would've shaken your head or said something like 'Not worth mentioning...' or some shit like that. But you didn't, which means you're still thinking about her. What's her name? Where'd you drive her?"

"Her name? Like I'm going to tell you that. It wasn't like I went out of my way or anything. It was just while I was doing my evening run to the farm." I shrugged and turned on the TV.

"Alright." He pulled out his cell phone and dialed...

"Hey. Who'd Mikey drive when he went out to the Crashaw place today?" he said to his phone.

"Ass," I mumbled.

"Yeah, I thought so too..." he continued speaking to his phone. "I don't know... I haven't seen him with any girls in a while either! ... Alright man... you take care. Thanks a lot."

When he hung up, he said to me, "Justin says you drove the youngest Crashaw. Haley, maybe? He wasn't sure. But we know the word in town is she's very pretty. What happened to that woman you were dating from Hooterville?"

I laughed and nearly spit out my drink at his remark because I knew it wasn't called that and all the men around here just called it that because they went there to pick up women.

"You know that's not the actual name of the town, right?"

"Yes. It's... actually, I've called it Hooterville so long that I don't remember the real name."

Laughing at his ridiculousness, I corrected him, "It's Homerville."

"Ha. Yeah, that's right. What happened to her? She was mildly attractive. Wasn't she?"

"I suppose. But she bored me."

"Everyone bores you," he said, taking a drink of his beer and shaking his head. "But I'm supposing that this little chick is a bit more exciting?" he asked, raising his eyebrows up and down. "Want to tell me about her?"

"Maybe she is, but you know my situation. It's not like anything could happen. Plus, she seems very young, and she's going to be a doctor; I very much doubt she would want me anyway." I shrugged and leaned back, taking a drink, and turning the channels on the TV.

"I would give it a go," he said, nodding.

"I'm not you."

"Besides, it's not like farming is your full-time gig. Does she know who you are?" he asked, pointing to my college successes on the far wall.

"I have only known the girl a few hours. And no, I don't intend on telling her any of this because I'm not taking it any further. I can't."

"Suit yourself. Can I have a go?" he laughed.

Quickly turning my head in his direction, I snapped, "When I'm dead and I can't kill you, only then can you speak to her. Until then, don't even look at her."

"I don't get it. You're not dating her. Hell, you're not even asking her out. What's the deal?"

"She's too good for you," I said, standing and walking away to take a shower.

"But not for you?" he asked as I walked down the hallway.

"She's too good for me also."

While I was in the shower, I let her face run through my mind the whole time I let the cold water pound onto my back, and I tried to come up with a way to distract myself from the undeniable attraction I was having for this woman. But my efforts came up empty-handed as I thought about the ride to Crashaw farm and how she peeked out from under her blonde hair as it fell over her blue eyes.

"You can't," I said to myself as I stepped out of the shower and wrapped a towel around my waist. "It wouldn't be fair to her. What if she got attached?"

Thinking about the comment for a moment, I thought how irrational it seemed and laughed slightly at myself. "Don't kid yourself, Mike. There's a reason you're 38 and unmarried with an estranged family. Maybe just one fun night for the hell of it."

As soon as I said that to myself, I was reminded exactly why it wouldn't work out.

"Hey man, you alright in there?" Luke hurried to the bathroom when he heard my struggles.

I looked down at the toilet and saw the blood, flushed it down, and answered, "Yep. All's good."

But I knew that all wasn't good, and so did he.

Three

"Goodness! Who on earth could that be?" I heard my mother holler from her bedroom. Glancing over to the clock on my nightstand, I noticed it was about 7 am and I wondered what was going on. So, I tossed on a robe and followed her down the hallway and that's when I heard what she heard: the gentle pounding on the front door.

I paused at the top of the stairs to watch as she opened the door, curious to see who was there.

"I apologize for disturbing you so early Mrs. Crashaw, but I realized that I'd left Hadley's luggage in the back of my truck last evening."

Just as Michael said that he looked up to me, smiling slightly at the sight of me in only my fluffy bathrobe.

"Oh, um, good morning, Hadley. Sorry to disturb you. I have your luggage," he said, picking it up and extending his arms.

Smiling at his courtesy, I motioned for him to bring it upstairs to my room, "You didn't need to trouble yourself, but go on and bring it up here, if you don't mind."

"No trouble at all."

He set the bags to the left of the door inside my room and paused to take a look around at the room I'd grown up in, glancing around at the walls that still had the terrible green and pink floral wallpaper, horseback riding trophies, and ribbons, and the fair ribbons I had from baking pies and mixing jams with my mother. But then he paused on one that I didn't figure would catch his attention and he asked, "Is this when you decided you wanted to be a doctor?"

I walked over to where he was standing in front of my first-place trophy for the state science fair for my project on germs and viruses and common household illnesses.

"No. I did that project because I already knew I wanted to be a doctor. I had decided long before that."

"I see," he replied looking over to a few pictures on my dresser. "Well, I'll leave you to your privacy now. They're predicting a pretty severe winter storm, so I thought I'd get an early start on the animals and your father's barns today."

"What about your job?" I asked before I realized I had no right to intrude on his personal life.

"Don't worry about me."

"Wait!" I blurted out without any idea why or reason to do so.

He turned around in the doorway and looked back to me without responding, but his eyes smiled, waiting for me to continue.

"Would you like some pancakes?"

"Sure. That sounds nice."

With wide, happy eyes, I told him to meet me in the kitchen and that I'd be down after I got myself into more appropriate clothing, and he nodded pulling my bedroom door closed behind him, but not before turning his head back to say, "Nice duckies."

"What?" I asked, scrunching my face, confused.

He pointed to my mother's fluffy white robe that had yellow rubber duckies all over and said, "The robe... you look... cute." Then he walked out.

I looked down at myself in the robe not thinking I looked at all cute in that oversized bathrobe and trying to see it from a man's perspective. "He is so perplexing," I thought as I looked down at myself and walked to my luggage to pick out something to wear.

After dressing in jeans and a red sweater, I hurried down to see him chatting in the living room with my father.

"Good morning, Daddy. Did you sleep well? How's your back doing on that old mattress? Mama said it's been bothering you again."

When I said that, Michael walked out of the room and back up the stairs, and I figured he was going to the bathroom and thought nothing more of it.

"Back's been acting up again and the doc says that the arthritis is only going to get worse now that I've been taking that medication for my cholesterol."

"Are your levels raised again?" I asked, walking into the kitchen in order to peek at his medication bottles which were kept in the cupboard above the sink.

"That's what the doc says. But you know what?" he said while I stretched up as far as my short legs would allow me to reach for the bottles that were on the far top shelf.

"What's that?" I asked him, still stretching for the bottle that was far out of my reach.

"I don't know why it's so raised because I'm doing everything that doctor..." he continued talking.

"Let me get that for you."

"Goodness!" I exclaimed as Michael reached over me and pulled the bottles off the shelf, placing them down in front of me.

"Sorry to surprise you. But I came in here thinking you were going to be making those pancakes," he said with a wink. "Why don't I help?"

"Oh. Um, no need," I said as I quickly glanced through the medication bottles. But as I was doing that, he turned and pulled the mixing bowl off the top shelf and turned to remove the flour canister lid and dug a measuring cup down inside before I could make it over to him.

"I'd like to help," he said as I approached.

I took my mother's old patchwork, tattered apron, and tied it on, then I handed him the old, plain white one and said, "Let's get to work. Daddy's going to be wondering where breakfast is."

He walked to the fridge to get some eggs and I'll admit that I watched him walk across the room for my eyes' pleasures, and I'd do it again in an instant. But I can't say what it was about this man that I found so alluring because, at the same time that my eyes were finding him so good-looking, my mind was finding him so undesirable.

"How many should I make?" he asked, glancing up at me as he was still rooting around in the fridge.

"Well, it's just the four of us..."

"Right, then lots," he replied.

With his hands full of eggs, butter, milk, and more things than I could count, he walked over to the counter where the dry ingredients were and got to work.

"How do you like your eggs?" he asked as I pulled up a bar stool.

"Don't go through the tro..."

"Nonsense. Now, don't sass me. How do you like your eggs?"

Blushing, I looked down, covered my face with my hand, and answered, "Scrambled is fine."

"With cheese?"

"If you insist."

"You shouldn't hide your face, you know," he said as he started pouring the pancake batter onto the griddle.

"What do you mean?" I asked and looked up to him as he quickly moved back and forth between the griddle and the pans on the stove where he was frying bacon and sausage. My eyes were satisfied at the sight, but my heart and mind were battling for the best of me and telling me that it would do me no good.

"I mean that you have such a pretty face and such beautiful eyes that it does you no good to cover them up, especially with that sassy mouth."

"Oh..."

He paused his motions and looked over to me. "Hadley, you're beautiful, intelligent, and sacrificial. You could easily be a man's downfall."

Then he resumed cooking.

"What on earth did he mean?" I thought, unable to decide if it was a compliment or an insult.

"Thank you for the compliment," I finally said, shaking myself from the shock that consumed me.

"It wasn't a compliment," he returned.

Widening my eyes, I walked over to help him set out the food, but he leaned in and whispered, "I think you're very beautiful, but I also think you could take a man down in the blink of an eye. I'll learn to watch myself around you." Then he grabbed up the platter of pancakes and walked away.

Stunned, dazed, confused, and a whole mess of other emotions I couldn't even begin to describe, I only stood there trying to compose myself, until he said, "Hadley, want to bring those eggs? Your father is going to be expecting breakfast."

Instead of doing what he asked, I just stood watching him, admiring his messy, dark blond hair, soft but masculine features, and tall and muscular physique which he'd gotten from working the many farms his whole life. But mostly I was enraptured by his ocean-like blue eyes that kept glancing in my direction, though not willingly— I could tell— and he was fighting the urge to give in to his desire for me.

"Hadley," he said once more, a bit more frustrated this time.

"Hm?" I said with a mouth full of eggs.

"Are you going to stand there eating at the counter or are you going to help me with the rest of breakfast?"

Without saying anything, I picked up the pan of eggs and walked over to him but discreetly took my fork with me, and when I laid the pan on the table in front of where he stood at the table, I dug my fork into the eggs, taking another bite, and tipping up on my toes to whisper in his ear, I said, "I'm going to do both."

He exhaled heavily and closed his eyes.

"Why don't you let your parents know it's time to eat?"

"I can do that."

I skipped away, hoping to entice him, but I wasn't sure why. Was I interested in him? No. Did I want him? Yes.

Walking away to get my parents, I glanced back and saw him sitting at the table, elbows digging into the wood, forehead cradled in his hands.

He was sitting just that way upon our return.

"Well, isn't this the sweetest surprise!" my mother exclaimed when she saw breakfast made.

"Did Hadley put you up to this, Michael?" Daddy said, sitting down at the table across from him, Mama sitting down next to him, leaving me to sit next to Michael, which I now believe was their plan all along.

"No, sir."

"Well then, what's all the fuss?" she asked.

"No fuss, ma'am, just a kind gesture," he returned.

"Mama, Daddy, just enjoy your breakfast and stop getting yourselves all in a tizzy! You need to just accept when someone does something nice for you! Michael wanted to do it!" I scolded, pointing to the food and their plates. "Now, load up your plates and eat. He needs to get a head start on all the work before the storm starts."

"Goodness, child. Don't you talk to your mama that way," she said, piling her plate with eggs and sausage.

Michael smiled and leaned over to me, whispering, "Yeah, don't you talk to your mama that way." Then he winked and reached out for some pancakes and began talking to my father about work on the farm.

"Well, I better get outside. It looks like that storm could begin any minute now," he said, taking his plate to the sink, washing it off, then reaching for a towel and drying it before placing it back in the cupboard.

"Don't you worry about the mess now. Hadley will clean up," my mother so willingly offered up to him.

Grinning at me as though he knew how to push my buttons, he replied, "Of course. Thank you, Hadley."

Surprised that he didn't say something snide, I only nodded and watched him go to take his jacket off the rack and slip on his boots. Once he was outside, I hurried to the door to look out the window to watch him walk across the field to the big, red barn. However, my efforts in ogling were quickly thwarted when he looked back to the house and almost saw me in the window before I ducked down.

"That was close!" I thought.

"Hadley Lynn!" Mama hollered out.

"Yes, ma'am?" I asked, standing to turn and look at her.

"What in heaven's name are you doing?"

"Nothing."

With that, I gave up my efforts and went to clean up breakfast. However, I was certain to glance out the sink window every so often to see if he was on the side of the house. To my great dismay, he was not.

Once the dishes were finished, I hurried upstairs and threw on a warm jacket, scarf and gloves, boots, and a hat, then I went into my father's closet to look for gloves, a hat, and a scarf. After which, I raced downstairs and out the back door, hurrying to find him.

"Michael!" I yelled when I saw him on the big tractor preparing for the snow that was coming.

Surprised to see me out there, he stopped the tractor and jumped off, running over to me.

"What are you doing?" he asked, slightly out of breath from hurrying across the field in the cold air.

"It's cold," I said handing him the cold weather gear I brought out.

He half-smiled and wrapped the scarf around his neck, pulled the hat over his ears— his messy blond hair puckering out slightly from the bottom— and slipped his reddened fingers into the gloves. Then he looked at me and lifting his hand to my face he said, "Thanks."

"You're welcome. We've got to make use of the time we are given. Right? I saw someone in need," I said, winking.

When I turned to walk away, he called out, "Hadley, wait."

"Yeah?" I asked, turning to face him once more.

"Come. I want to show you something."

Excitement was the emotion of the moment. It was for me at least as I took his hand and he led me across the field and helped me up onto that big tractor, positioning me in front of him with his hands on my waist as he held onto me tightly each time the tractor shifted gears and jerked just slightly, and he would lean forward and say, "Don't worry," as though I wasn't raised on a farm. But it was sweet nonetheless.

"Where are we going?" I asked as he drove that tractor off the field and to the far edge where the woods were.

"You've lived on this farm your whole life, but I bet you've never seen this," he replied, turning it off, jumping down, then extending his hand to help me down.

"Why haven't I seen?" I asked, staying put on the tractor while he stood there waiting for me.

"Are you always this unwilling?"

"Maybe."

"Just come on," he said, reaching his arm out again.

I finally surrendered and jumped out to him, slamming onto him, which I don't think he expected.

"OW!" he yelled out as he slammed onto the ground and me on top of him.

"Oh, don't be a baby," I teased. But he didn't say anything in response as I stood next to him but took a moment to recover as he held his right side near his ribs, and for a moment I thought I'd injured him until he stood and brushed himself off.

"Let's go," he said, holding out his hand.

Taking his hand, I followed willingly, and I looked down to our tracks in the already falling snow, feeling like those were the imprints he was leaving in my heart and if I didn't undo it quickly, it would be unable to be undone.

"Almost there," he said parting the trees, walking down a path, pulling me along.

"Where are we going?" I asked, but just as I said that he showed me an abandoned hunter's shed.

"Are you coming?" he asked as he began climbing up the ladder.

"Oh, um... yeah." I followed behind.

Once we got up, I saw that he already had it set up with supplies—blankets, a battery-powered lantern, and a few flashlights.

"What do you do up here?" I asked.

"Look," he said and pointed to the field on the opposite side of where we'd climbed up.

When I saw the reason for his visits, my eyes were beginning to see this man in a new light, which was frightening my heart. My eyes were already enjoying this perplexing man and the last thing I needed at this point in my life was to captivate my heart.

"They're beautiful," I said looking out to the field full of deer.

"This is where I relax," he said and moved away and leaned against the back wall.

I looked out the window a few moments more before positioning myself next to him and covering us with a blanket, which I felt was a boldly intimate move, but he didn't seem to mind.

"So, you come here to relax... what else does Michael Radcliff do with his time?"

Sighing deeply, inching me closer with his arm around my hip, he said, "Not much."

"What's your daily life like? You know I'm preparing to be a doctor, but what do you do?"

"This."

"Farming?"

"Life."

When he said that, I looked over at him and noticed an expression of sadness cross his face.

"Michael? What does that mean?"

"I live."

Knowing he was hiding a deep secret, I didn't push further. Instead, I rested my head on his shoulder in the perfect position to relax my whole body against his, and he moved his arm upward, wrapping me in his embrace.

"You're going to be my downfall, Hadley Crashaw."

Four

"Hadley," he said, brushing the hair away from my face.

Yawning, I leaned up and stretched out my arms, but then my whole body shivered at the cold, and I realized we were still in the hunter's shed!

"We didn't..."

He chuckled slightly and smirked before saying, "No. Although..."

I whipped my head around in his direction to scold his man-thoughts. But the moment I looked at him, I retreated my sharp tongue. His blue eyes were piercing my heart and I couldn't hold back any longer— I leaned in. Taking his face in my hands, I moved closer—practically sitting on his lap—and wrapping the blanket around us once more, I took his lips fervently in mine.

He returned the kiss eagerly and wrapped his arms around me, pulling me onto his lap and tightening the blanket around us. But as the kiss became heated and I started moving my hands under his shirt, he pulled back.

"I shouldn't..."

"I'm sorry," I replied, moving away.

"No. I just meant that I'm... never mind."

He pulled my face back to his and planted his soft lips against mine again, moving his hands up my back and entangling his fingers into my hair.

"What am I going to do with this?" he mumbled through our kiss.

"What do you mean?" I asked.

"Well, I mean... surely, you know I'm going to be sneaking into your window tonight, and I'm going to have to come up with a very reasonable explanation for Mr. Crashaw on why my truck is still going to be here in the wee hours of the morning, you know, other than for the reason that I'm fooling around with his very cute daughter."

Giggling, I moved back to his lap and said, "Well, I am a grown woman... a consenting adult."

"How old are you?" he asked, leaning me back, sprawling out next to me and pulling the blanket over us.

"Don't you know you should never ask a girl that?" I replied.

"Well, I'm pretty sure I'm a good bit older than you, but I don't care. I'm giving in." He resumed kissing and allowed his hands to explore.

Mumbling, not wanting to interrupt the best kissing session I'd ever had, I said, "I'm 29."

He pulled away and looked into my eyes for a moment and said, "29? You don't look it. I thought you said you are a medical student?"

"I said I'm an oncology fellow. There's a difference. I've graduated from medical school. Now I'm focusing on the practice of oncology."

"I see," he said as he moved his kissing to my neck and gently brushed my hair away from my ear in order to plant some kisses there. "Hadley?"

"Yeah?"

"As of this moment, 38 is a pretty good age for me."

"Hm... Maybe I should take you inside and then ask you how you feel about being 38 tomorrow," I said, as he moved back to look at me.

"I'm good with that. Unlock your window."

After returning the tractor to the barn, he moved his truck and I went in to unlock my window, telling my parents goodnight but also that Michael was heading home for the evening. But it wasn't as simple as that with my nosy parents.

"Is he going to be okay driving back to town with all that snow coming?"

"Yeah. I'm sure he'll be fine," I said, trying to walk away, but she stopped me again.

"He has that 4-wheel drive on his truck, Martha," Daddy chimed in.

"Oh, that's right, Gary," she replied. "Did he leave to go home? Perhaps you should invite him to the spare bedroom. I hate to see him driving in the storm all the way to town."

"As far as I know, he left. I'm heading up to bed. Goodnight," I said.

"Goodnight."

I raced out of there and to the stairs, moving up as quickly as I could and into my room where I saw him sprawled out across my bed, arms tucked under his head.

"Window was unlocked. You've done this before?" he asked, grinning at me.

"No. Mama was probably cleaning. Sorry, it took so long. They want to know if you are going to make it home with the heavy snowfall we are getting. Where'd you park your truck?" I asked, joining him on the bed.

Kneeling up next to me, he extended his hand to me as he started removing my shirt, kissing down my neck as he did. "Behind the cow barn. My truck has 4-wheel drive. Your father never goes back there. He shouldn't see it."

"So sneaky."

As I started working on his shirt, he paused me and said, "You don't make this a regular habit, do you?"

"Fooling around with my daddy's farmhands? Or getting involved with men I barely know over Christmas vacation?"

"Both... I guess."

"No. But you're pretty quick and willing. Maybe I should ask you the same question." I lifted his shirt over his head and was awed at his perfect form but I noticed a scar just a few inches under his left clavicle bone and I couldn't help but ask.

"What happened?" I said, extending my index finger, and tracing the scar.

Hesitant in his reply, he looked down to my finger, brought it up to his mouth, and began tracing my finger along the outer edge of his lips instead, kissing each one as he said, "Don't be Dr. Hadley right now. Just be the Hadley that is driving me absolutely crazy and out of my mind."

"Oh... which Hadley is that?" I moved just slightly so he could lay back as he unfastened his pants and kicked them off, revealing his boxers."

"Christmas trees?" I asked.

"Just trying to be festive. I didn't know anyone except me was going to be seeing them." He winked.

"You didn't plan this?"

"I hoped, just a little."

"Oh?"

He moved to lay me back and as he was kissing around my neckline once again, he said, "You are very beautiful."

After pausing there for a moment, I thought about his previous comment.

"Michael, which Hadley is driving you crazy?"

He looked me in the eyes and answered, "I date around a lot, but I don't stay with women too long because I get bored. Not too many women can strike my fancy on first notice. But the moment I saw you, I was captivated. But then you spoke and I needed you even more. A beautiful doctor with a sassy mouth? My every dream come true."

I giggled slightly and brought his face up to kiss my lips.

"You say you date a lot of women. Do you always take advantage of the farmer's daughters?"

He didn't answer as he reached beside the bed to his jeans pocket for the foil packet, and when he looked back up at me, he said, "Well, I had to go to the drug store today, if that says anything."

He leaned in to kiss me, ready to make use of that foil packet. But I interrupted his advances once more, much to his frustration, when I said, "How did you know you were going to need it? You didn't know I was going to come out to the field and interrupt you."

Slipping it on, looking me in the eyes, and entangling his fingers in my hair, he whispered in my ear, "From the moment you spoke and the second I saw you, I knew you were going to be my downfall. If I'm going to be brought to my knees by you, I'm going to at least be prepared for battle."

Giggling, I whispered back, "Well, you're having quite the time during the fight."

"You have no idea," he groaned from where his face was buried in my chest, finally making use of that foil packet.

"Hadley," he whispered a good while later as he was holding me against his chest, running his fingers along my spine.

"Yes?"

"You are my most satisfying downfall ever."

"What are you saying?" I asked as he moved beside me.

"You are the Delilah that just took down Samson."

"I don't understand," I said, planting a kiss on his shoulder.

"I love you. Anything you want, it shall be yours."

"You hardly know me."

"I know what I want and I know what I like. I've never had a woman captivate me the way you can. You've conquered me."

He moved over me once again, wrapped his hand behind my head, and laid a passionate kiss on my lips before trailing them downwards, as he was enjoying himself, my thoughts bounced back and forth between realizing that I might actually love him too but also understanding that he wasn't right for me.

"How do you know it's love?" I asked as he was reaching into his jeans pocket again.

"I just do."

The next morning, I woke to hear my mother buzzing about in the hallway, so I sprang up, concerned that she knew what I'd done last night— not like it was her business anyway—nevertheless, I didn't want a commotion.

Looking to my left, I saw an empty bed and wondered where on earth he would've gone.

"Michael?" I whispered.

Upon hearing nothing, I said it a bit louder, "Michael? Are you here?"

Still hearing nothing, I decided to throw on the bathrobe and investigate.

"Michael?" I said, walking into the hallway, and glancing to the bathroom and other rooms. When I didn't see or hear him, I walked downstairs.

"Michael!" I called out when I saw him sitting in the living room with my father as though it was no big deal at all for him to be there in the wee hours of the morning.

"Hady!" my father said as I walked into the living room in only that bathrobe. If only he'd known what Michael and I were doing just hours before, his reaction would've been a little different, possibly.

"Morning, Daddy, Michael. I didn't know we had company so early. I better get dressed," I said with a quick wave and a movement of my eyes to let Michael know I wanted him to follow me.

"Well, he never left. Apparently, we got quite the storm, and even his 4-wheel drive couldn't make it out."

"Is that so?" I replied, trying my hardest to hide my smirk. "Where'd you sleep?"

"My truck," he said with a wink.

"Oh."

"Now Michael," Mama said, walking in. "No need for you to do that. You should have stayed in the room next to Hadley. If you need to stay tonight, that's where you'll be." Then she walked out, and I turned to go back upstairs.

Plopping down on my bed the moment I entered, a thousand thoughts panicked my brain. "What in the world are you doing?!" I berated myself. "He is a farmer! You are a doctor! It will never work! Stop this and stop this now! There is a reason you left this area!"

"Hadley?" he knocked.

"Come in."

He quickly shut the door behind him and then he just stood, leaning against the bedroom door as though he wanted to say something, but he didn't. He just stood.

Finally, he said, "Nice duckies."

Rolling my eyes, I responded, "It's not mine."

"I figured as much. But I'm not talking about the robe."

Blushing slightly, I pulled it tighter around myself.

"It's okay. No need to feel embarrassed. I've already had a good see of them. I quite enjoyed myself. In fact..." He walked over as I was gripping the robe, and he whispered, "I think it's time I had another look." Then he moved my hands and began unknotting the robe, but we were interrupted when my mother pounded.

"Hadley?"

"Ugh... Just hold on," I said and put my finger to my lips to signal for him to be quiet.

"Yeah, Mama?" I said, only cracking the door.

"Did you see where Michael went? I was going to offer him a shower."

"I didn't. But I can tell him. I'm sure he's outside. I'll be sure he gets a towel."

I shut the door and locked it. When I turned around, he was on the bed.

"How about it?" he asked.

Laughing slightly, I stripped off the robe and watched his eyes widen satisfactorily. "Fine," I said, "But you're going to have to be a bit more discreet this morning."

Pulling me to him, he said, "Quiet as a church mouse," and he held his pointer finger over his lips whispering, "Shhh."

Five

Upon first meeting Hadley Crashaw, I knew she was going to be a weakness for me, but I didn't quite know how difficult it was going to be to resist that woman. Watching her walk out to the field with her father's gloves, hat, and scarf for me, pulled out a soft place in my heart that I hadn't visited in a long time. I crumbled.

"Do you want a shower?" she asked as she ran her fingers through my hair and we lay on her bed together.

"Eventually," I replied, leaning in to kiss the sensual part of her neck that only made me want to keep going. I pulled away because I could hear her mother in the hallway—mood killer.

"Did you mean what you said or was that just a sex line?" she asked.

"What did I say?"

"You said you love me."

"I said that out loud?!" I thought. "Shit."

"You know, um…"

She sighed. "It's fine. I figured it was just 'guy talk' for 'I think you're so hot.' No explanation is needed. I've heard it all before."

She stood and walked over to the closet, and I watched her the whole way— taking it all in— but reality hit me, and I called out to her.

"Hadley, no. That's not it at all."

Half-dressed, she turned to look at me.

"Then what is it?"

"I've got kind of a complicated situation."

With disbelief written all over her face, she spat, "You mean like you're a baby daddy? Or you don't pay your child support? Or do you have a girlfriend and I'm a one-night stand? Are you a felon wanted in fifty states? Which one is it?"

Laughing softly at her overreaction, I said, "It's nothing like any of that. I just..."

"Are emotionally unavailable? Yep, I've heard that one too." She turned her back to me and continued dressing. But just a few moments later, before I could compose my thoughts, she said, "Look, Michael, I'm not asking for a committed relationship, only the truth." She turned to look at me once more and saw that I'd stood to put my jeans back on, and when I glanced back at her, I saw the slightest of smiles cross her face.

"Happy to see me go?" I asked.

"No. Just thinking that you have a nice butt."

"Heh. Thanks. Yours is nice too."

"Are you going to be working on the farm today?" she asked.

"I'll be back a little later. I have some things I need to take care of first."

"Your real job?" she asked, walking over to me where I looped my belt, and she ran her hands up and down my chest.

"Yeah."

"What is it you do?" she asked, pushing me back onto the bed sitting on my lap, putting her arms around me, resting her head against my chest.

"Oh, um..."

"Is it terrible? Are you like a club bouncer or a bartender or something?"

"No."

"Why can't you tell me? Are you embarrassed?"

"Not at all."

"Michael?" She looked up to me, kissed my cheek, and asked me again, causing me to surrender, "What's your real job?"

"I'm a real estate attorney."

She let out a slight gasp and said, "What?"

"That's what I do. I'm an attorney."

"I never would've guessed."

"Because I also work on farms?" I asked.

"I don't know. I think because you don't give off the attorney vibe." She teased, poking my chest and teasing my beard stubble with her fingers. "You're a little rough around the edges."

"That's true. Does it change your opinion of me?"

"No. I think I admire that you've kept it a secret and don't flaunt your intelligence. I like that." She leaned her head in against my chest once more and said, "I'm not sure how to feel about you, Michael Radcliff. You are..."

"Not what you were expecting?" I asked, finishing her sentence.

"More. More than what I was expecting, and that is dangerous for me."

"And dangerous for me."

I wrapped my arms around her for a few moments and tucked her head tightly against my chest in the palm of my hand, wishing to keep her there forever, though I knew that wasn't possible. How could life be so cruel? Where had Hadley Crashaw been all my life? These past two years I needed a Hadley Crashaw yet I didn't have her. Now the last thing I needed was her and here she was. How backward life seemed.

"I have to go," I said, tilting her face up, and kissing her once more. "I'll be back this evening."

"Maybe ..."

"What?"

"I was just thinking that maybe I could sneak into your window tonight." She gave a wink, biting her lip flirtatiously.

"Oh. Um... I don't know."

"Why not?" she asked, looking curious.

"I'll take you with me when I leave here after finishing up this evening. But..."

"But what?"

"What are your parents going to say when you're not here in the morning?" I asked, skeptical of their reaction to her absence.

"Don't you worry about them. The only thing you need to worry about is clean sheets because I have brothers and I know how men are, and bottled water, and also get your playboys out of my eyesight. I don't want to see that."

I laughed at her forwardness and replied, "You are so high maintenance."

Walking to leave her bedroom, I turned just before closing her door and said, "Hadley?"

"Yeah?"

"I meant it."

"Wait!" she hollered and followed me out.

"What?" I asked when she raced into the hallway after me.

"Didn't you want that shower?" she asked, pointing to the bathroom door, pulling on my hand to follow her.

Sighing deeply, knowing I needed to go to the office and deal with some cases I had left on my desk but thinking of her lathering up in the shower, the thought of her won over in my mind.

"Yes," I said and closed the bathroom door behind us.

"It's 11 o'clock," Gayle, my middle-aged and grandmother-looking secretary said when I walked into my office two hours late. "I overslept," I said, reaching my hand out for the mail.

"Woman?" she asked, smiling, as she pushed her falling glasses up onto her nose

"Gayle, why do you always say that when I'm late?"

"Because it always is, sir. And I know it is this time."

"How could you possibly know that?" I asked, shuffling through the mail.

"Well, because you showed up wearing the same thing you left in yesterday, sir. And because I tidied up your office for you."

The realization of that had just occurred to me, that I didn't change back into my business wear, and that I was still wearing farm clothes. But as for her reference to my office, I wasn't certain.

"Shit, Gayle."

"Was she that disorienting?" She laughed.

I ran my hands over my face and said, "I think I love this girl."

"Oh, sir. I've never heard that word from your mouth before and I've been your secretary for 10 years!"

"I've only known her for a day. She's... something."

"Would you like me to send her a gift?" she offered. "This is big news!"

"Gayle, you know my situation. I can't."

"How does she feel about you?" she asked.

"I don't know. But it doesn't matter. I have to end it," I said, walking away toward my office.

"Alrighty. Well, you got a call this morning from a John Crashaw..."

"What? Why?" I asked and turned back to face her.

"Something about his family's farm. He left you this number." She handed me a piece of paper and I immediately walked into my office and picked up the phone, dialing John.

"May I speak with John Crashaw please?"

"This is John. Who is this?" he asked.

"This is Michael Radcliff, the attorney..."

"Oh yes! Thank you for returning my call..."

From that point, he explained to me the entire situation of the Crashaw farm, having no idea that I already knew some of it from his sister's perspective.

"I would like you to see what you can do for the deed. I hear you are very good at what you do. I've already arranged for the deed to be sent to your office later this week."

"If I understand correctly, all of your siblings own the farm jointly. Is that true?" I asked.

He then explained that their grandmother had signed the whole of the farm onto them with the condition that when their parents became too old to care for it, they would then inherit it.

"My parents signed it over to us just last year, but we had no idea of the under-clause."

"Which is, of course, that you have to sell it in its entirety. I'll take a look and see what I can do. I'll be in touch with you sometime next week."

Dropping my face into my hands, I knew that there was nothing my firm could do for that farm. Complex legalities of that nature were only sorted out through rewriting and sale. They needed to sell it.

"Mr. Radcliff?" Gayle buzzed the intercom.

"Yeah?" I answered.

"You have a call on line one. It's Dr. Ramirez."

"I'll call him back."

"That's what you told him last time..."

"Thanks, Gayle. Back to work."

As soon as she hung up, for some reason, Hadley crossed my mind, and all I wanted to do was drive out to that farm. But I couldn't. Instead, I worked for a little while on some open cases that I needed to type up final reports for, then I browsed the internet for a little while looking for a gift I could give to her. With no success, I tidied the pile of papers on my desk, grabbed up my jacket, and walked to the door.

"Leaving so soon?" Gayle asked.

"I have a few errands to run."

"Can't get her off your mind?" she replied.

"See you tomorrow."

"No, you won't."

Stopping in the doorway and turning back to face her, she said to me, "It's Thanksgiving. I suggest you stop by the drugstore and get some more of those foil packets before you completely lose your mind. I left the one that fell from your jacket pocket yesterday in your desk drawer."

Shaking my head, I walked to the door and hollered back, "Enjoy your holiday. Tell your husband to save me some of that pie!" Then I waved and walked out.

"Pull yourself together!" I berated myself as I sat in my truck, forehead leaned against the steering wheel, thoughts raging in my mind over why I was falling so hard for Hadley in such a short amount of time. "She's just a pretty girl. What is with you?" I said and banged my head forcefully against the wheel and without even realizing it, I hit my head so hard that I left a gash about the size of an inch above my right eyebrow.

"Damnit!" I hollered out as I jumped out of the truck to let the dripping blood pound onto the pavement instead of onto my jeans.

As quickly as I could, I pulled off my t-shirt and held it against my forehead to stop the bleeding.

"Fantastic," I said, now realizing I needed to go home before I headed up to the farm.

"Michael?"

"Hadley?" I spun around to see her pulled up next to me in her mother's old Cadillac.

"Why are you standing out here in the cold without a shirt?" she giggled. But then she saw me holding my shirt against my forehead and she put the car in park and got out. "What happened?" she asked, removing the shirt from my forehead, and looking at the gash.

"It's no big deal. I just bumped my head," I said with blood dripping down my face.

Disbelieving, she opened the door to her car and pointed for me to get in.

"Nonsense. I'm a doctor and I'm going to fix you. Now let's go."

I got in and watched her walk around to the driver's side, feeling like the irony of every part of this situation was too much to be real.

She drove to the drug store where I frequented and I couldn't help but smirk slightly at the thought of us being in there together.

"What's so funny?" she asked as she took my hand and pulled me along to the first aid aisle, as I still held my t-shirt tightly to my forehead.

I reached into my jacket pocket and felt the last condom that hadn't been used and I replied, "Just smiling at the irony."

She stopped immediately where we stood and she said, "What is it with you and 'smiling at the irony'? Why can't you just tell me what's so funny?!"

"Yeesh," I replied, feeling a little on the defense, "I'll tell you."

Taking her up another aisle, leading her away from the first aid, I showed her the aisle I would've returned to later had I not been an idiot.

Blushing with a smile, she said, "I see. Well, don't let me stop you," and she pointed over to the racks for me to continue.

But I motioned to my forehead as though we needed to fix me up first.

"Oh right. Let me take a look." She waved her hand for me to lean forward and she removed the t-shirt and said, "The bleeding has stopped and it's coagulated."

"What?"

"It'll be fine until I can patch it up for you. Go get our goods. I'll get your bandages and meet you up front." She waved with her hand, winked, and walked away.

My gaze followed her the whole way down the aisle and I couldn't take my eyes off how she swayed her hips from side to side with each step she took. When she disappeared around the corner, I looked back at the rack of so-called sex protection and picked up a box then whispered, "What kind of protection are you? I don't need you. You're nothing more than a temptation. I need protection *from* sex."

"What are you doing still over here?" she asked looking down the aisle to see me still standing at the boxes of no-good.

"Oh, uh..."

"Just come on. I have what I need to get you all fixed up." She waved and smiled, and at the sight of her beautiful eyes, I was all hers.

"That'll be $34.78," the cashier said as I reached for my wallet and pulled out my credit card.

"Aren't you Hadley Crashaw?" she asked, smiling wryly and looking at me.

"Yes. Why?"

"No reason. Enjoy the rest of your day." She handed me the bag and said, "You know, Mike, we sell super packs."

Hadley laughed softly as I took her hand and practically dragged her out to the car.

"You shouldn't be so uptight," she said, as I opened the passenger's side door and sat her down.

"I'm driving."

"What? You could have a concussion!" she protested.

"Just mind yourself and stop being so sassy."

"At least let me put your bandages on first. You're oozing," she said, holding her finger against the once again dripping blood. "Here..." She reached into the drug store bag and took out a cleaning pad, wiping my cut with it, and then she started placing gauze pads on it.

"How did you do this?" she asked.

"I bumped my head."

"Obviously, smart ass. Specifically?"

Instead of answering, I gave in to my temptation once again as her delicate fingers moved across my face... fixing me.

"I missed you," I mumbled from our kiss.

"It was only a few hours."

Ignoring her, I pulled her over to my lap and started giving in to my urges even more.

Straddling my lap on the driver's seat, she held my head in her hands and said, "I missed you too, which is why I offered to run errands for my parents."

"Hoping to see me?" I asked, pulling her back in for a kiss.

"Or more."

Excited at that statement, I said, "I have somewhere we can be. Buckle up."

I hurriedly drove us back to my truck and said, "Come with me," leading her out of the car and into my office.

"Not here to work, Gayle. Hold my calls," I said as I pulled Hadley past Gayle's desk and down the hall to my office.

"Top drawer on the left!" she hollered.

"Take lunch!" I yelled back and heard her exit the front door a few moments later.

"I'm assuming I'm not here as a client?" she asked, sitting down on my desk, biting her lip flirtatiously.

I shook my head, stripping off my shirt, and beginning the search immediately for that little foil packet Gayle had left. Once I found it and pulled it out of the drawer, she asked, "Why is that in there?" and she stood off the desk with a horrified look on her face.

"No! No... Yesterday, I came to the office right after the drugstore. When I shoved the condoms in my pockets— some in my jeans and jacket— one fell on the floor and my secretary found it when she was cleaning up."

"Oh. A much better explanation than I'd expected."

"What did you think? That I'm some attorney who brings his clients in here and gets freebies on his lunch break?"

She laughed and shook her head. "No! I just figured you like hookers!"

"Ha. Not my scene."

She walked over to me and asked again, "How did you hurt your head? The truth."

After kissing her for a moment and lifting her onto my lap where I was sitting on my desk, I said, "I was very frustrated about something and I purposely smacked my head against the steering wheel."

She gasped and held her hand to my forehead. "What could make you so upset?"

"Love."

Six

My intention of going to town to run errands for my parents was two-fold. I admit that I was hoping to see Michael, but I also wanted to get away from that farm for a few hours too. Living in the city for the past 12 years has left me with the ability to only handle small doses of country life before I break. However, I didn't know I would actually succeed in my ventures.

"Why are you so distressed?" I asked.

"Why do you say that?" he replied.

I touched the bandage-covered gash on his face but didn't comment again, and he held my face in his hand for a moment and said, "I don't want to hurt you. I've never felt like this before."

"Then don't."

"I fear it isn't so simple." He lifted me and laid me on the floor, unfastening my jeans, whispering, "Rock my world."

Quickly taking him by surprise, I pushed him down next to me by his shoulders and said, "You won't know what hit you."

Then I started kissing on his chest, but I paused by the scar on his chest and the doctor in me couldn't resist.

"What happened? Farm Equipment?" I asked and planted a gentle kiss on it.

"No."

Looking up into his eyes from where I had my chin rested on his abdomen, I could tell he wasn't going to answer me, so I continued kissing up his chest to his lips and whispered, "I'll figure you out eventually."

"Good luck." He flipped me back over, taking control once again, and I realized that even though I might not have been able to figure out him, he wanted to spend his time figuring out me.

"Michael?" I asked a good while later.

"Yeah?" he answered, standing to get dressed.

"What are we?"

He looked down at me quizzically and said, "People."

"Okay, funny boy. I mean, like me and you, are we just having sex, or are we more than that?"

Horror was the immediate expression on his face, soon followed by contemplation, before he said, "What do you want us to be?"

"I don't know. I'm just wondering what will happen when I go back to Chicago in a few weeks?"

"I think you just answered your question," he said, slipping on his boots.

Standing and quickly dressing, then walking over to him as he moved to walk out, I hollered, "Michael!"

He turned back just before he grabbed the doorknob.

"How did I answer it?" I asked.

"You're going back to Chicago and I'm staying here. Feelings or no feelings, how could it work?"

He walked out. But I quickly hurried behind, demanding more of an explanation. However, I felt embarrassed at the sight of the secretary who had returned to her desk and was smiling at me as I walked past, surely knowing what we had been doing in there.

"Hello, miss..."

"I'm Dr. Hadley Crashaw. Nice to meet you."

"Mr. Radcliff didn't mention you were a doctor," she said with a small grin.

"He mentioned me?" I asked, feeling a bit mortified.

She shrugged and said, "Have a good holiday."

"Holiday?!" I thought. She was right! Tomorrow was Thanksgiving, which meant my brothers would be coming in later. It also meant I wouldn't be seeing Michael! Unless...

I hurried out the door to ask him about his holiday plans.

"Hey!" I hollered out, rushing up to him where he stood at his truck.

"Yeah?"

"What are you doing for Thanksgiving?" I asked, taking his hand, and pulling it to my lips.

"Don't celebrate it."

"What are you talking about?" I asked, looking at the sadness in his eyes. "It's an all-American holiday. Everyone celebrates Thanksgiving."

"I don't."

Thinking for a moment as he climbed into his truck, I said, "Why don't you come and have dinner with us?"

"What? Why?"

"Because everyone celebrates Thanksgiving."

The words he said next crushed my very soul...

"No. Everybody doesn't. I haven't had a Thanksgiving dinner in 10 years."

Looking either pained or shamed— I wasn't sure which— he turned to climb into his truck to leave. But I reached for his arm and said, "Are you heading to the farm?"

"In a little while."

I nodded and then walked away to the car, noticing he was watching me as I left. Feeling frustrated and bemused over his refusal to open up, I finished the list my parents had given me, beginning with the bank.

"Hi," I said, walking up to the clerk.

"How may I help you?" she asked.

"I need to talk to someone about a late notice for this account." I handed her my parents' over-due mortgage for their retirement home that they'd purchased a few years ago, not believing we'd have such a hard time getting rid of the farm.

"You want to pay it?" she asked.

"No. It's accumulated too much. I need to see about getting some help stretching out the past due amount."

"You'll need to go see Mr. Bryant right over there. I'll let him know you're coming."

She pointed across the building to a closed office door and picked up the phone, and I walked away and to the chair immediately to the left of the door.

As I was waiting, Michael walked in, and I hid my face behind my hair as he walked past, trying to discreetly watch him as he went up to the teller. I did my best to listen in on the conversation, but I couldn't hear anything. I only watched and noticed how confident he seemed without being proud. The teller was obviously flirting with him, but he didn't seem to care, which sent my admiration even further through the roof. He handed her some papers and then his ID, and she made some remarks to him about whatever was on the documents he'd given her.

But then as he waited for her to turn and finish his transaction, he glanced my way, noticing me, and then his entire demeanor with the teller changed and he was all of a sudden very flirtatious, or so it seemed. She started smiling, biting her fingernail, and giggling, and for a moment I thought he was flirting with her to purposely cause a stir in me. But then they both quickly looked my way and Michael filled out what appeared to be one of those account transaction slips but I couldn't tell which kind it was, and he finished just as Mr. Bryant emerged.

"Dr. Hadley?" Mr. Bryant said, as my jealousy over the flirtatious conversation Michael was having with the teller seared my heart and changed my mind about him, just a little.

"Please come in," he said.

I stood to shake his hand, followed him, and sat down to discuss the particulars of the payments that were past due, but he beat me to it.

"You're here about the missed payments on your parents' mortgage?" he asked.

"Yes. I know they are severely delinquent. But I can pay two months today and one of my brothers can pay some more..."

"I'm looking at the account here and I don't see that it's still delinquent at all."

"What? That's not possible. We received a statement in the mail. I know my parents don't have the money..."

"Someone paid on the account only today. It's been settled," he said, looking through the computer in front of him.

"I don't understand," I replied.

"Well, there was a sum just added to the account, paid in the amount of $7,879, and it was added just a few moments ago, actually."

"I have to go," I said and hurried out of there.

The realization occurred to me that Michael's flirtatious behavior was all with a motive now, and I ran outside to try and catch him because I knew that it was his doing.

"I know what you did!" I yelled as he walked to his truck.

"I'm now the one in the dark and you are not," he said as he kept walking.

But I yanked on his shoulder as I caught up to him and forced him to face me. "Did you flirt with that teller so she would tell you why I came to the bank?"

He shrugged and kept walking.

Tears started falling and my mixed emotions for this man were no longer feeling so mixed but now were seeming much more focused.

"Michael!" I yelled, sniffling and wiping my now overflowing tears.

He walked the few steps back over to me, took me in his arms, and said, "Maybe I did."

"Why?" I asked as he pulled my face up, wiped my tears, and kissed my nose.

"I need to do good with the time I have on this earth."

"Is it possible to fall in love in only a day?" I asked.

"I'm trying to figure that one out," he said, kissing me.

"When you do, let me know."

"Believe me. You'll know."

He enclosed his arms tightly around me, kissing my forehead as I said, "How do we ever thank you for something like this?"

"Save me a seat next to you tomorrow."

Happiness crossed my face as I reached my hands up to his face pulling his lips to mine, and I said, "Aren't I having a sleepover tonight? You can just be my guest."

He half-smiled at my comment and said, "Go home and get your things. I'll be out to the farm soon." Then he kissed me and got in his truck, and I watched with desire as he drove away.

The whole drive back to the farm all I could think about was Michael. While I wanted to continue whatever this was what was happening between us, I felt like we led such different lives that ultimately it could never work out. My plans after fellowship were not to come back to this area, or even to Colorado, and I was quite certain that he had no plans to leave either. We hardly knew each other and we hadn't had any real heart-to-heart conversations. But I did know one thing: no one had ever stirred this type of emotional discord in me ever before. I mean, I'd had boyfriends— and lots of them—but Michael was the first one that I'd ever considered using the word "love" with. Was he a boyfriend? Did I want him to be a boyfriend? I supposed that was the contemplation happening in my mind at the current moment. I did care about him and I was undeniably attracted to him. When he wasn't around, it seemed like he was the only thing that occupied my mind. Although it shouldn't be a huge indicator in a relationship— though it did seem important enough for me— he was strikingly good-looking and was truly the best sex I'd ever had. There were so many positives that it was hard to convince my mind that there were any pitfalls to being with him whatsoever.

As I got closer to the farm, I remembered him calling me his "downfall," and I tried thinking about what he'd meant by that.

"Did he not want to be with me?" I thought.

"Maybe he has another relationship that he isn't ready to admit?" I continued my internal reflection.

My thoughts continued similarly to the house, and I pulled into the garage, pausing briefly before I exited, considering that all of this had been a mistake.

"Maybe I need to end this..."

"Hadley? What took you so long?" my mother called from the house as I exited the car.

"Sorry. I ran into Michael in town and we got to talking..."

"Oh?" she asked.

"I invited him to Thanksgiving dinner."

"I'm glad you did. Poor thing. He just seems so lonely all the time," she said, motioning for me to come inside.

"Why do you say that?" I asked, dropping the groceries on the table and hanging up my jacket.

"Well, he's a well-known attorney in town..."

"Wait, a second! I asked if you knew anything about him!"

"I thought everybody knew that!" she said, brushing me off with a wave of her hand.

"What else do you know about him, Mama?" I asked as she started putting the groceries away.

"Well everyone in town knows that he has some kind of disagreement with a family member. A sister possibly? I'm not sure, but I know that he doesn't talk about it at all and it's the reason he lives where he does now."

Curious about that, I asked, "What do you mean?"

"Well, I'm not sure. It's only hearsay, but I think that the sister is holding his house hostage because of something that happened." She shrugged and kept putting away the food.

"Mother! Do you have any idea the trouble it is to drive out here to this old farm?" Ethan said, walking in the front door as Mama and I were finishing the groceries.

"Hi, Ethan!" I hollered, rolling my eyes.

"Hady? What are you doing here?" He walked into the kitchen and looked around, taking off his jacket and tossing it onto the table.

"Hello Mother," he said, with a peck to her cheek.

"Ethan," she said, hugging him. "Please don't complain. You're much more handsome when you're not complaining. You still look just like your father."

"It is a dreadful drive."

"E, why don't you just not come then?" I asked. "I'm sure your prissy, what's-her-name, high-maintenance girlfriend would do just fine staying in LA anyway."

"We broke up."

"Shame. She was certainly marriage material."

"Yes, because every man you've been with has been bring-home-to-Father material."

"Would you two stop?!" Mama yelled.

Ethan walked over to the living room door and said, "I'm stopping; but it's the holidays, I'm allowed a few jabs at my sister." Then he went into the living room where our father was watching TV.

"Brothers…" I mumbled.

"You've got four. I'm surprised you haven't learned to live with them by now."

"Well, Mama, they've tortured me my whole life. I just feel lucky that I don't live near any of them. Although, I do miss Jack's little ones now and then. Will he be joining or is he going to Maggie's parents?"

"They're coming. I asked them to come since they didn't join last year. They live so very close to the other grandparents and I don't get to see Helena and Carter that often."

Pulling the sack of potatoes off the bottom shelf of the pantry closet and setting it down on the table to the right of where she was sitting, I said, "Well, we are going to have a full house then. We'd better get started." And I handed her a potato peeler as I started rinsing.

Seven

Being invited to Thanksgiving dinner at the Crashaws' place nearly pushed me past the little bit of what I was still holding together. Hadley was becoming probably the sweetest, kindest, and most sincere woman I'd ever known— all in only just over a day or so.

After I left the bank, I went by my house to be certain that it was decent enough for a guest, but I was interrupted.

"What's going on with you?" Luke asked, walking inside.

"Nothing out of the ordinary," I replied as I tossed empty beer bottles and containers of Chinese food, pizza boxes, and other garbage, into a trash bag. "Just cleaning up."

"That's out of the ordinary. What's the special occasion?"

"No occasion, just thought I'd clean. Now, if you don't mind, I need you to get the hell out of my way so I can get going. I need to be out at the farm."

"Time to go see your new nighttime interest?" he said, walking over to the fridge to grab a beer.

Instead of replying, I smiled slightly and turned away so he wouldn't see the satisfied look on my face.

"That's why you're cleaning, isn't it? She's coming here? Are you bringing that Crashaw girl to this house? That's an awfully big step. Are you serious about this girl?"

"No. I'm not."

"You're not bringing her here or you're not serious about her?" he asked, turning and walking from the fridge to the couch, turning on the TV.

"Both. Move your feet," I said as I swept underneath him.

"Right. Michael Radcliff never cleans, well, except when you hired that hot cleaning lady last year."

I stopped sweeping and frustratedly said, "I'm just tired of living in a mess. It's not about Hadley."

He looked contemplatively at me for a moment, then he stood and walked to the door as he said, "Yep, which is why you called her 'Hadley.' Old man Crashaw is gonna kill you, man. See you later, lover boy." He walked out and I got right back to cleaning, wondering if Hadley's dad really would freak out if he found out about us. It probably held some truth. I mean, I knew if I was a father and I found out my daughter was messing around with my farmhand in secret, I would probably take my Remington shotgun to him in the middle of the hay field. But I wasn't sure how Mr. Crashaw would react. Nevertheless, I wasn't giving Hadley up. I would take that Remington right to my chest. Though I wouldn't admit it to her, I was fairly sure I loved Hadley. And I didn't know how because I'd only known her for two days. But I did know that she was the most beautiful person I'd ever met, inside and out.

Having never felt love before, I also didn't know if what I was feeling was true and I felt like I needed to test it. When Hadley asked me if it was possible to fall in love in only a day, I was still testing that theory inside my own heart. But as I returned to my house and looked around the space, all I could think about was her face, her arms, her beautiful body, her lips, the way she held me, the way she spoke—all of it. Everything about her made me want to never let her go and wanted to beg her to never let me go.

As I finished cleaning, I sat on the couch and rested my head in my hands to think about the emotions running through my mind. Did I love this woman? Possibly. Could I do anything about it? No. Did I want to keep up with what I was currently doing with her? Very much so. And I planned on doing just that.

However, life always has other plans.

"This is Michael," I answered my cell on my way out to the farm not too much later on after I cleaned the bedroom and washed my bed sheets. "He's where? Right. Well, I can come later...This is who? Oh. I understand... I'll be right there."

I hung up the phone and climbed onto my Harley, heading for the hospital.

"Luke Brady please," I said to the ER receptionist as I walked in.

"Are you the friend I was alerted about? The uh... Michael Radcliff?"

Thinking I would need to show ID, I pulled out my wallet and flashed my ID at her. "Yes."

"Yes or no would have been sufficient," she said. "He's in surgery right now, but there's a sheriff who is outside his room and would like to speak with you. Go along that way right there." She pointed to a long corridor to her left and pressed the button to allow me entrance.

When I approached his room, I saw the Sheriff standing outside and became curious about the situation with my very best friend.

"What's going on, officer? Is he in some kind of trouble?"

"You're the attorney?" he asked.

"Yes."

"Luke is in very critical condition and he's off to surgery right now, but he is under suspicion of driving under the influence and the other vehicle involved had no survivors."

Sighing deeply, running my hands over my face, I began pacing the hallway in front of his room.

"Involuntary manslaughter?" I asked the officer.

He nodded, and I leaned against the wall to think about the laws that I hadn't dealt with in a very long time.

"I'm a real estate attorney," I thought. "I'm not a defense attorney."

Looking over to the sheriff, I said, "I have a call I need to make." Then I walked out to the waiting room to try cellular reception, which was hard to get anywhere in this area.

"Mr. Crashaw? Hi. I'm sorry to do this to you, but I have a bit of an emergency and I won't be able to make it out to the farm this evening. But I'll make up the time. Could you let Hadley know... Oh, if she's right there then yes, I'll talk to her."

"Hi, Hadley. I'm so sorry, but I have to change our plans... I'm so sorry.... It isn't about you... A friend was in a terrible car accident and he's in the ER. I'll miss you...I'm still hoping to come by tomorrow though... That's sweet of you... I have to go. Bye."

She seemed disappointed, which pleased me because I was saddened at the thought of not being able to meet up with her tonight. I stood at the lobby window for a moment and watched the snow begin to fall, and I thought about how angry I was at Luke, even though I didn't want to be. But I was angry because nothing could ever seem to go right in life. I supposed it was selfish of me to feel that way when my best friend was fighting for his life and would now be on trial for involuntary manslaughter. Selfish I might've been in my thoughts about Hadley, but my days were numbered and I was trying to make the most of them.

When I returned to his room, the nurse was there to speak with me, preparing his room for his arrival.

"Are there no relatives that we should call for Mr. Brady?" she asked.

Now feeling very concerned, I answered, "Why?"

"The doctor will talk with you momentarily." Then she walked out.

Unknowing what else to do, I took a seat in the visitor's chair inside his room and just let my emotions take over me, wondering what his current condition was like.

"He's the only friend I have," I thought. "If I don't have that idiot, I have no one."

A little while later in the middle of my internal despair, there was a knock at the door, and when I looked up, all my hopes and dreams skyrocketed out of control.

"I know that I have no right to intrude on your personal life, but when you said that you had a friend who had been in a terrible car accident..." she said, peeking her head inside.

"Come in, Hadley," I said, motioning for her to come over to me as I stood and hugged her. "Thank you for coming."

"Where is your friend?" she asked, looking to the right where the bed should've been.

"Surgery. He is in critical condition. They called me because they suspect he was a DUI and now they are going to charge him with involuntary manslaughter."

"Oh... what can you do?" she asked.

"I'm an attorney."

"For real estate," she remarked, walking over to see if the chart was left outside the door. With an old country hospital like this, they were still in the dark ages and used paper charts.

"Yes, but as a doctor, you went to medical school, correct?"

"Yes."

"You know about the entire body and all its functions, correct?"

"Correct."

"But you just specialize in a particular interest?"

"You've proven your point," she smiled flirtatiously.

Walking over and standing behind her, putting my hand on her waist and brushing the hair away from her neck, planting a kiss there, I said, "I know the law very well. I'm just not a defense attorney. If needed, I could help a guy out. Luke is my best friend."

She turned to face me, and said, "Have you talked to his attending physician yet?"

Feeling a bit bewildered, I said, "No. Why?"

She didn't answer, but she walked out and to the nurse's station, demanding answers, and I smirked at her sassiness.

"Excuse me," she said to the nurse at the desk, forgetting she wasn't an attending doctor there.

"May I help you?" she replied.

"I would like an update on the progress of Room 15."

"And your relationship with him?"

"Um... I'm his best friend's girlfriend, and I'm also a physician at Regions."

'Girlfriend?!" I thought, panicking. "Calm down. She only said that for answers... but be honest with yourself, you like the sound of it."

My internal thoughts went a little haywire at the thought of her using a formal title for herself, though I knew she did it for information. But most of me didn't care that she used that title for herself and kind of likened the thought.

She listened to the update from the nurse before stepping back into the room.

"Girlfriend?" I said as she walked back over.

"Please don't be freaked out. I knew they wouldn't give me information if I wasn't closely involved with the patient. Being your 'girlfriend,' I thought would be enough, which it was since you were here."

"What did they have to say about him?" I asked, standing and offering her my seat. But she refused and kept standing with her back against the wall.

"Well, he is out of surgery, but he isn't allowed visitors yet. He's in recovery and she said that we should move to the upstairs waiting room." She extended her hand to me as I stood to follow her out and she said, "Calm your fears. Your friend is going to be fine."

Knowing I wasn't able to do anything for him just sitting there, I suggested that we go to the cafeteria and grab a bite to eat and she thought that was a good idea.

"I'm used to hospital food. But I must say that I'm used to a higher class of hospital food," she teased as we went down the elevator.

"I'm certain it is. Those big city hospitals have all the resources that we do not. But I'm sure you'll do just fine for today."

Brushing her finger under my chin, she laughed softly and turned to grab a tray off the pile as we entered, looking to the soups. "Hm... should it be creamy broccoli or chili?"

"Get the chili," I said while I grabbed a ham sub from the sandwich pile and started loading it with toppings.

"Why?"

"Because I've seen you eat and I know you won't finish it all, which means I'll get to. Chili is man food. Creamy broccoli is crap."

She laughed again, moving closer to me, taking my hand in hers, and gently kissing it before saying, "Chili it is." Then she took the biggest bowl filled it up to the top and tossed a bunch of the saltine crackers on her tray.

"Is this together?" the cashier asked.

"N..."

"Yes," I said, and handed her my credit card.

Once we found a seat, she scolded me.

"You shouldn't have done that."

"Why?"

"I have money."

"I know. But you're my girlfriend," I replied, winking.

She rolled her eyes and crumbled up her crackers into the chili.

"Tell me about your friend."

"Luke?" I asked, taking a bite.

She nodded.

"Well, he's an ass most of the time. He doesn't know about you. So, when you walk into the room, he's going to be shocked and give you a hard time, but give it right back to him. He's used to that. Don't let him mess with you. Give him your sass. He's a generally good guy. But he does like to cause a lot of commotion."

"He's your best friend?"

"My only true friend," I replied, realizing how distressing it was for me to think about losing Luke. To distract my mind, I reached over and took a bite of her chili, and she half-smiled at my actions.

"I'm sorry, Michael," she said and moved around the table to sit next to me, putting her arms around me, resting her head on my shoulder, and kissing my cheek. "You must feel so helpless." Then she pulled the chili across the table to us and handed me the spoon.

I nodded to acknowledge her words and took another bite of her chili as she sat there—arms around me, fingers stroking my hair, lips dancing across my jawline. But what she didn't know and probably never would know was that I felt even more helpless when I was sitting there wrapped in her arms. She had so much control over my heart that it was dangerous for her, me, and everyone. I was Samson; she was my Delilah. She was my beautiful downfall.

When we returned to the waiting room, Luke's doctor came over to speak with me.

"You're the closest thing he has to a family?" the older male doctor with balding white hair asked.

"Yes. He's my best friend, but he's like a brother to me."

Looking to Hadley, he said, "And you are?"

I spoke up so she wouldn't feel awkward. "She's my girlfriend. She's a doctor at Regions hospital in Chicago. I asked her to be here."

"I see. Why don't you come with me? I'd like to speak to you about your friend's situation in private."

Hadley didn't look at me when he said that but glanced down to the floor, which I felt gave the indication that something very terrible was happening to him. I took her hand and walked in silence behind the doctor.

We sat down across from him at his desk and his demeanor immediately confirmed my worst fears.

Leaning forward, hands clasped together on his desk, he said, "Luke suffered massive internal bleeding when he was thrown from his motorcycle."

"Where was the bleeding?" Hadley asked.

"We repaired a hemothorax, a cardiac tamponade, and several other lacerations of smaller organs."

"But if he is still in need of repair, I'm assuming he must have an intracranial hemorrhage that you still have to fix?" She persisted in her questioning, which I admired, and I admit that it was a bit sexy to see her in doctor mode.

"He does have head trauma, but we fear it will not be as easy as we were hoping."

"Why not?"

"His body is in a coma."

Eight

So badly, I wanted to help Michael and his friend Luke, but there wasn't anything anyone could do. Comas are one of those medical mysteries that require waiting and patience.

"Come home with me," he said, as we walked to the elevators.

"Are you sure? You've had a traumatic evening."

He stopped and turned to face me as he stepped onto the elevator and said, "I've never been more certain of anything in my entire life. Come with me." Then he took my face in his hands, kissing me as though he was never going to get another opportunity to do so. I enjoyed every second until the elevator doors closed on us, and I giggled as we stepped on and resumed kissing.

"So..." I said the moment I got the chance.

"Yeah?" He mumbled and began moving his hands up my shirt.

"What are we?" I reached my hands up around his neck and dug my fingers into his hair, pulling him tighter against my lips.

"You're my Christmas present. Santa got my letter."

Feeling as though his reply gave me a bittersweet prick in my heart, knowing he wasn't making a commitment to me but also knowing he was saying that he was making some kind of declaration for me without saying more, I didn't push him to make it more; I moved my lips to his cheek and then whispered in his ear, "You're mine too." And he moved his fingers to gently grasp mine as we exited the elevator.

I was surprised when we got to the parking lot to see that it wasn't his truck he was climbing into, and I was sure to comment on the sleek Harley Davidson motorcycle.

"You don't strike me as a motorcycle kind of guy."

He grinned and said, "Every man needs a toy."

Handing me a helmet, he said, "I don't make it a habit of taking passengers. Consider yourself special."

Then he pulled out some special goggle-type glasses to put on his face, which concerned me because then I realized that I was wearing his helmet.

"I can't wear your helmet," I said.

"I'll be fine." He reached his arm back, scooting me closer to him, getting a nice feel of my behind as he did, which only made me clutch onto his jacket all the tighter when I reached my arms around him and buried my head onto his back, as he revved the engine and took off. While he drove through the back, country roads, I maneuvered my arms up under his vintage leather jacket to get a firmer grasp of him, and I think he knew I was a bit nervous because a few times he tilted his head to glance back my way and then finally asking, "You okay back there?"

"I'm perfect," I said, squeezing him tighter.

When indicated Hollow, he stopped at the intersection in front of the big, blue house and he paused for a moment to stare.

But I couldn't help but ask, "Do you know the history of that house? Last time we came past it..."

He sped off before I could finish, making me know that he had some type of involvement in it, and I was beginning to wonder if possibly it involved the family member my mother had mentioned. I didn't want to be nosy, but I was incredibly curious. My instinct was telling me it was an ex-lover...

When we pulled up to his house, the sight surprised me quite a bit, not being at all what I'd expected now that I knew he was an attorney and was probably somewhat wealthy. The house was small and old with a brown, wood exterior that needed replacing. He didn't maintain the grounds very well, and there was no landscaping. The small front porch had paint chipping and needed new cement poured. The sight was very shocking for a man of his status in society.

Walking inside was even sadder. The décor was old and very plain. To me, it looked like he purchased the house and moved in without redecorating. There were no pictures of loved ones or friends, or nothing personable at all, except maybe one sign that said BUDWEISER, which I thought might've been his.

"Make yourself at home. Are you hungry? I can order something to eat," he said, as I walked over and looked inside his empty fridge, noting the case of beer and pizza box but nothing else. Saddened at the sight, I said, "Don't fancy cooking?"

"Well, I spend most of my time at the office, or these days I've been enjoying your mother's good food," he said with a grin.

Walking back over to him, I said, "She is quite the cook. I wasn't always as thin as I am right now. You may not have liked me when I was growing up."

"Oh?" he asked, kissing around my neck, and moving my hair. "I find that very hard to believe."

"Well, I liked Mama's cooking a lot," I admitted.

"Hm... I'm fairly certain I still would've found you very irresistible. You're a little skinnier than the girls I normally date. But I can't help myself. I'm finding you irresistible. There's something about you."

"What is it?" I asked.

He lifted me into his arms. Then he whispered, "I don't know entirely. I caught a bug and only the doctor can fix me. Now, about that food..."

"I'd like a spinach and mushroom pizza," I said and then kissed his cheek.

Almost able to hear the groan from inside him as he ordered, he said, "Hey Pat, it's Mike. I need a pizza delivered..." As he was ordering, I began glancing around his living room at all his things and paused to look at his movie choices, curious to see if he forgot to stash away his pornos— not seeing any. I knew he'd been sneaky enough to hide them away. But I took notice of some of my favorites there like The Shawshank Redemption, The Green Mile, The Matrix, and even to my surprise, To Kill a Mockingbird.

"Finding anything you like?" he asked, sneaking up from behind.

"Oh!" I exclaimed.

"I know what you're doing, clever girl. I don't have any."

Quickly, I stood to face him, and he continued speaking with a sly smirk on his face, "Even if I did, do you think I would leave them out for you to find? Hell no. I'm not an idiot. You already told me to put my playboys away."

Taking his hand in mine, I asked, "Did you do that too?"

"No. Didn't need to. I'm not that kind of guy."

Tilting my head, waiting for him to continue, I didn't say anything in response. So, he finally said, "When I have the desire, I just go to the bar and find a date."

Thinking it was an incredibly better option than the previous, I said, "Always a different girl?"

"Dr. Hadley, don't you know that patients never tell the truth about these things?" He lifted me and carried me over to the couch, sitting me down on his lap.

"Yes. But doctors know it's not the truth, which is why we always make a note of something like 'patient is a big, fat liar' and then write down what we think, especially when it comes to womanizing men like you." I winked at him as he began lifting my shirt over my head and replied, "I'm not a womanizer. I just prefer real women to the fake ones on the DVDs and magazines."

He laid me back and pulled a foil packet out of his pocket, but I interrupted.

"Dr. Hadley wants to know how many women. What's your number?"

"We are doing this right now?" he groaned.

Sitting up slightly, I said, "Well, I need to know..."

Interrupting me, he held his finger to my lips and said, "I know what you're going to say, and it doesn't matter because I'm always protected. Plus, you should've asked before we did this the first time. If I was a problem, it's too late for you."

"I suppose you're right. But if I guess will you tell me?"

He chuckled at my persistence and nodded.

"Seven."

He laughed, so I knew I was far off. After thinking about the fact that he was 38 and wealthy, I guessed again.

"25?"

He didn't remark this time, so I figured I was a little closer, if not right on the mark. But his face was saying something that I couldn't read and I thought he might've been a little uncomfortable with the conversation, so I changed the subject. "What do you have to drink other than beer?"

"Water. I followed your instructions. Bottles are right over there." He pointed to the table in the kitchen, and when I stood to walk to get one, he asked me to bring him a beer from the fridge.

"Feeling stressed?" I asked when I looked back over to see him leaning forward, resting his elbows on his knees, face buried in his hands.

"I'm worried about Luke."

I handed him his beer and he said, "Pretty doctor, tell me about comas. What are the chances he's going to be okay?"

"Well, when I was in medical school, I had to do rounds in ICU and I worked with several people in comas. From what I've learned and have been taught firsthand, I know that it's uncommon for them to persist beyond several weeks. What you see on TV and movies isn't real. If they do remain prolonged, most people in that condition transition to a prolonged vegetative state..."

"What does that mean?"

"It only means that the longer he remains unconscious, the less likely he is to wake up. However, most people who are in a comatose state wake up within weeks, not months."

"What about people who have a case like his? What is the likelihood that he will wake?"

"It's very hard to say at this point. I haven't seen his scans and I don't know the extent of his brain damage. I'm unaware of what needs to be repaired."

He looked away from me, taking a chug, wiping his mouth on his sleeve. For a brief moment, I thought I saw his eyes watering and I wanted to comfort him, so the only thing I could think of to do was offer my advice.

"Michael? What if we transfer him to my hospital? I know some really great ICU physicians and I could help keep better track of his care there. We could have him life-flighted into Regions and you could stay at my apartment with me. I can arrange everything."

At my words, he just sat frozen like a statue for a moment. Then he stood, held out his hand, and said, "Keep talking doctor to me, but let's go to the bedroom."

His bedroom was nothing I'd imagined it to be, not with his relationship history. Fairly simple, with just a mattress and box spring on a bed frame, a gray blanket and white sheets, and one dark wood bedside table and matching dresser, I felt like he went out of his way to be simple.

"Come here," he said, pulling me along to the bed, sitting down and lowering me onto him. But like my usual self, I couldn't help but be nosy when I saw a picture on his bedside table of a very pretty woman with blonde hair.

"She's very pretty," I remarked, pulling away from his kiss, pointing to the woman in the frame.

"I don't want to talk about it."

"Okay," I said, still looking at the woman, thinking she was probably a relationship gone bad. And in my bad habit of intruding, I asked, "Was she important to you?"

"Yes."

He pulled my shirt over my head and positioned me so that I couldn't see the frame anymore, but my curiosity still wanted to know more.

"Did you love her?" I asked.

"Very much, but not in the way you are thinking."

"Oh?" I asked, pulling his shirt over his head, and for the first time I noticed he had a tattoo of a snake on his right side, stretched across his ribs.

"How did I not notice this before?" I asked, inspecting the serpent-like tat that had snake venom dripping and the words CURSED inside the venom.

"I'm not sure. The lights have always been dimmed until now. Perhaps that's how." He shrugged and unfastened the hooks on my bra.

"What's it mean?" I asked.

"That woman? She was my mother. She died 10 years ago and ever since, my life has been cursed. She was an angel from God, but since she died, the serpent has taken over and I'm not so sure that there's any good left to life now."

Thinking his statement was the saddest thing I had ever heard in my entire life, I only moved closer, placed a gentle kiss on his lips and made the next few minutes of his life worth living for.

"My god, Hadley..." he said as he laid on his bed and stared at the ceiling.

"What?" I answered, pulling his blankets over me, moving closer.

"My mother never would've approved of you," he chuckled, and looked over to the picture, setting it back up from the position he had placed it in, face down on the bedside table.

"Do you always do that?" I asked.

"What?" he asked.

"Make Mama kiss the bedside table," I giggled.

"No need. I never bring women in here."

"Oh?"

"I have another bedroom." He leaned in and kissed my forehead, then he said, "Pat's delivery boy probably left the pizza on the porch. I better go check."

He stood and slipped on his boxers and jeans, and I watched every moment that he moved. Even though he had a rough and tough exterior and wasn't as refined as the city men, there was a good possibility I was more attracted to him with each second that passed than I'd ever been to any city man I'd ever dated. I found it a great compliment that I got to see his bedroom when other women did not. I wondered why I was so set apart and decided I would ask as we ate pizza.

He walked out and I looked around his bedroom for something quick to throw on, when I saw a t-shirt and sweats tossed over the chair situated in the corner. After giving them a quick sniff test, I decided to just toss them on. Then I joined him in the kitchen, where he was opening the pizza

"Why am I special enough to see your bedroom when you don't take your other girlfriends in there?" I asked, taking a bite of pizza, as he put in a movie.

"I guess I just don't look at you the same way. For the same reason I let you wear my clothes." He smiled and pointed to me in his t-shirt and sweats. "You're causing me to think differently about relationships."

"What do you mean?"

"I told you already; you are my downfall."

Thinking on that for a moment, I said, "You said that, but I'm very much in the dark on that statement."

"I haven't seriously dated anyone in a while before you and hadn't planned on it. But now you're causing me to think differently..."

"About what?" I interrupted.

"Life."

He walked over, sitting down next to me on the couch, and he asked, "Do you really think it's possible for us to go to Chicago with Luke?"

"Yes. I'll call the ICU and make arrangements in the morning. I have admitting privileges there since I'm a physician on staff. It may be a bit trickier since I'm not Luke's physician, but that's where you come in."

The happiness radiating from him was so evident that he didn't need to say thank you; I could see it in his eyes.

"And as for us?" he asked.

"Well, I have an apartment near the hospital and we will fly instead of taking the train. We'll book a flight from Denver and fly in as soon as possible. I have a roommate, but she won't care."

"A roommate? You strike me more like the live alone type."

"She's quiet and isn't around much. She's a chef and works long hours."

He nodded and walked over to the fridge, taking out a beer, and with a big swig, he said, "What will this roommate think of me?"

"Are you asking for your own personal gain or are you wondering what she is going to say about us?"

Annoyed at my remark, he said, "Has she met your city boyfriends to be able to give a comparison?"

"Yes. Feeling up to par?"

"Well, she's about to learn what country boys are all about."

Nine

"We don't need to go for Thanksgiving dinner," she said, her eyes following me to my closet while I found something appropriate to wear.

"I want you to be there. You're not missing it because of me. I already have enough explaining to do," I said, peeking my head out from around the closet door and extending my arm out to tantalizingly drop my towel onto the floor. She giggled excitedly at my actions though unable to see me from behind the door where she laid on the bed

"Believe me, Michael," she replied, "I'm not going to miss anything about arguments with my brothers. Holidays at my parents are never the best time."

Walking back out in jeans, carrying a button up shirt in my hands I said, "I think I went to school with your oldest brother, John."

"Yeah, I suppose you might've. He's about your age. But John is kind of a jerk. Did you talk to him?"

"No, not at all. I never played sports."

"Hm. What did you do in high school?"

Looking over to her wrapped up in blankets on my bed, I grinned at the thought of her being one of the girls I messed around with in high school, and for a brief moment I let that imagery pass through my mind before I said, "I got drunk."

She laughed, shaking her head at me. "I definitely could see that about you."

"What were you like in high school?"

"Hm... You know the girls you didn't date? That was me. I was the girl sitting in the library, trying to get as smart as possible because I wanted to become someone important and leave this town. I never dated..."

"Not even once?" I asked, walking over to the bed, half-dressed.

"Not until college. My first date was my freshman year of college with a guy named Sam. He took me out for ice cream and told me I was the prettiest girl he'd ever seen."

"He's right," I said, taking her face in my hands kneeling down in front of where she laid on the bed.

"Hm?"

"You are the prettiest girl."

After kissing her for several moments, and causing myself to wish I hadn't gotten somewhat dressed, I asked, "What's your father going to say about this?"

"I wouldn't worry about that. Daddy's just going to be happy that I'm not dating a guy from the city. I think he'll approve of you. In a way, he already has. I wouldn't care if he didn't. I really like you."

Thinking on that for a moment, I asked, "How many boyfriends have you had since ice cream Sam?" I asked with a peck to her nose.

"Not as many as you've had girlfriends."

"I'm sure that's true."

"That's a nice shirt. You look good," Hadley said, watching me button up my gray dress shirt not quite to the top and then roll up the sleeves to the elbows. Then I tucked it into my dark-wash jeans and added a brown belt, and after a bit of gel to my blond hair, I felt I could be seen at her family dinner.

"You clean up nicely. Now, if only we could do something about that stubble," she said, gesturing to my light beard.

"Leave it alone. It's not leaving," I replied, kissing her fingers.

The farmhouse driveway was full of cars when we pulled up, and Hadley hurried in the side door without me so she could rush upstairs to change out of my clothes without being seen, while I went to the living room to greet the family.

"Michael!" Mr. Crashaw called out. "Nice to see you! How good of you to join us. Let me introduce you to my sons. This is Ethan, Jackson, Nathaniel, and John."

"Wow, Hadley certainly is outnumbered in this family," I said, looking around to her four brothers.

"You know our sister?" Ethan asked.

"Only just recently," Mr. Crashaw replied. "They were introduced when Hady came back last week. Michael is a local attorney in town, but he is also helping maintain the farm."

"Oh! You're that Michael!" John said. "I would like to speak with you."

"Not now," Hadley said walking in, "I'm stealing him." She motioned with her head for me to follow, and I did immediately.

"Thanks for saving me."

"Anytime. My brothers are relentless." She took me into the next room over with the formal dining table and the piano, pushing me up against the wall, wrapping her hands around my head, and planted a few gentle kisses on my lips, before her mother walked in interrupting.

"Oh my!" Mrs. Crashaw exclaimed, catching us in the act.

Hadley pulled away immediately, looking to the floor, smiling, whispering, "Now we are caught."

"Don't worry, Mrs. Crashaw. I can explain," I said.

"You, explain?" she asked. "I want Hadley to explain!"

"Me? Mama?" she said.

"Yes, young lady."

"I'm not sure I know what you mean."

"Michael, please excuse us for a moment, if you would."

"Yes, Ma'am," I said before turning to walk out. When I stepped onto the front porch, I tried to listen carefully to what was being said, but I couldn't hear much beyond the scolding of Hadley's mother.

Feeling very uncomfortable with the whole situation, I decided to get in my truck and just head home. Thanksgiving wasn't for me anyway; it never would be.

"MICHAEL!" I YELLED, hurrying out to the porch after the ridiculous confrontation with my mother was over. Noticing he wasn't there, I raced down the driveway after him. "Michael!" I yelled, "Where are you going?"

"Home," he said, climbing into his truck.

"Why?"

"I don't belong here. Thanksgiving isn't my thing. Enjoy your meal." He closed the door without giving me the opportunity to protest, and then he drove away.

Sadness expended my entire being, and I wanted nothing more than to show him how much he belonged with me. I was so angry at my mother for her terrible behavior and I wanted to explain her actions to him. After thinking a bit on how I could do that, I gathered some things together, then I took my parents' Cadillac and drove to town.

Upon arriving at his house, I wasn't sure what I would say, but I thought, "I'm sorry," was a good place to start.

I walked up to his door, knocked, and prepared myself for the best damn apology I'd ever given anyone in my entire life, but shock consumed me instead as I was greeted.

"Hello?" said a moderately attractive, dark-haired woman.

"Is Michael here?" I asked.

"No. You are?"

"No one of significance." I handed her the basket and note I'd brought, and then I walked off the porch and went home wondering who in the world she might've been, assuming it was one of his many lovers.

"This, Hadley... this is why you don't get involved with men you barely know!" I scolded myself on the drive home.

My cell phone rang as I was approaching the farm; it was Michael. But my heart was so confused over the events that had just taken place that I couldn't answer it. I silenced it.

"So, Hadley has a thing going on with the new farm help?" Ethan teased at dinner.

"I went to school with that guy," John said, "He's a big-shot attorney now. What's he doing farming?"

"Haven't you idiots ever thought that maybe some people do things because they like it and it's not all about the money?" I sassed.

"How do you feel about it, Dad?" Jackson asked.

"Hadley is a grown woman. I can't tell her who she can see. Michael is a fine young man," he replied, looking to me.

My mother, on the other hand, had a different response.

"Well, I think it is a terrible thing, all this kissing in secret and nonsense. The way you kids date nowadays is a terrible thing. In my day..."

"Mama! We know!" I finally yelled.

"Hady, be respectful," my father said.

"I'm finished eating. I think I'll go upstairs." I excused myself and went upstairs to my room, but there was a surprise waiting in there upon my arrival.

"Goodness! What are you doing?"

"I got your basket," Michael said from where he laid on my bed.

"Where'd you go?" I asked, sitting down next to him.

"I don't do good with confrontation. I needed to think."

Stretching out next to him, teasing my fingers in his hair I said, "When I got to your house..."

"I know."

"Who is she?' I asked.

"A woman who wishes that we were still involved, though we will never be again."

"What's her name?"

"Sascha."

"Why are you no longer involved?"

"She asked too many questions," he said with a small smile, looking slightly down at me. "I appreciated the food. Your mother is such a fantastic cook."

"I made the potatoes."

"Yeah, I didn't really like those," he teased, tickling me, then kissing my nose.

Ten

Everything went relatively smoothly for transferring Luke into Regions. The trickiest part was that he was being held on involuntary manslaughter, but Michael worked on that right away and in only a few days, we had everything squared away.

"I don't know how you live here," he said to me as we exited the cab and walked up the stairs to my apartment.

"Why? What's so terrible?"

"All the people, the noise, the traffic... it's so busy. I don't like it."

Shaking my head, looking back at him as we walked to the third floor, I said, "I like it."

He dropped the bags onto the wood floor of my apartment once we entered and stood to take in the modern style décor with light gray painted walls and various pieces of art from Jennie's more classic taste, which off-set my taste for anything new and vibrant. As he started to move around and look at our things he said, "It looks like a chick's apartment."

Taking two glasses out of the cupboard and filling them with water before joining him on the couch, I replied, "Is that a compliment or an insult?"

"Neither."

"Well, okay then. I thought we'd have dinner and then go see Luke," I said.

"Sounds like a plan. Where do you like to eat?"

"I'll take you to my favorite."

"Alright. I'm sure it's fancy and very city-like with a feminine feel."

"Wrong," I said, standing and taking his hand.

When we got to the "L," he was without words.

"What's the matter?" I asked him.

"This thing cannot be safe. It can hardly be meeting any type of inspection," he said, pointing to the train station overhead.

"Ha! Says the man driving the crappiest truck I've ever seen! Quit being a baby and come on. It's fine. Hundreds of thousands of people ride the light rail every day. It's perfectly fine."

"Do you ride this thing?" he asked.

"Yes, when I need to get to the other side of the city. It's essential for city living. Now come on." I took his hand and dragged him up the stairs as I scanned my Ventra card for two passengers, entering the Orange line.

When he went to take a seat, I hollered, "Don't sit!"

"What? Why?" he asked, coming back over to me.

"I'll explain later. Just grab ahold of that bar right there and hang on."

Watching him ride the train was a humorous experience, and I'd never imagined him as a cautious person, not even in the slightest bit. But with each turn, bump, and speed change, he clung all the tighter to that bar.

"How are you holding up?" I asked, moving over to hold his bar as the train stopped at a station about 20 minutes later and passengers hurried on and off. I snuggled closely against him as the car quickly filled up.

"This is the worst experience of my life," he replied. "I don't know how you live like this."

Laughing slightly, I looked up to his frustrated face and said, "You must've gone to a university of some sort to get that smarty pants attorney's degree. Was it not in the city?"

"It was. But not in anything like this," he replied.

When we arrived at my favorite restaurant, he looked so startled by the appearance that he said, "You're not serious. Where are we really going?"

I laughed and responded, "This is it! Welcome to Portillo's! It's famous! C'mon!"

We walked inside and he paused to look around and the busy place, glancing up to the overwhelming menu.

"What do I order?" he asked as we stepped up to the register. "What's good?" he asked the cashier.

Smiling and looking to me, she said, "Newbie?"

I nodded and answered, "We'll have two dogs, a bowl of chili, and two drinks."

She punched it all in and the total came up on the screen. But when I reached for my card to pay, he had already handed her his card.

"Hey!" I exclaimed. "That's not right."

"What's not right?" he asked.

"You paid last time."

"That may be how you do things in the city, but where I was raised, men do the buying." And he looked to the cashier and signed his name, taking his card back.

"What's that supposed to mean?" I asked.

"It means that I like to do things old school."

"Ha!" I exclaimed. "Like how you sneak into my window or how you go through an entire box of condoms in one day? There's nothing at all old-school about that."

We walked to the end of the counter as they called out our number, and he looked at the tray with the hot dogs on it and said, "What the hell is this? That's not a hot dog! What's all of this slop?"

I picked up the tray and the cups and walked to get our drinks and said, "It's a Chicago style dog."

"What does that even mean?" he asked, following behind me.

"It's got lots of toppings on it, like a burger. Just try it. You're going to like it."

He took a bite and his eyes smiled at the taste, admitting that his Chicago dog was actually a good choice.

"It's good," he said, mouth full.

I took a bite too, and then a drink of my coke, and replied, "I know."

After we ate, we took the train back to my apartment and got settled for the evening.

Once he showered, he moseyed on out to the living room where I sat reading a magazine. But my eyes caught his image as he walked out in just some sweats, no shirt, and wet, messy hair, and I couldn't help but stare at him as he walked to the fridge to look for a drink.

"Definitely a chick's apartment," he said.

"What's that?" I asked.

"No beer."

He took a glass out of the cabinet, filled it with Jennie's red wine, then came over to me.

Sitting down next to me he finally asked, "So, why couldn't I sit on the train?"

"Because you could hardly even eat a hot dog that had more than ketchup and mustard on it."

"What's that got to do with anything?"

"You're very sheltered."

"I am not."

"Are."

"What does this have to do with the train?"

"Some of the things that happen on that train would make you vomit."

"But not you?" he asked.

"I'm a doctor. I have seen things you wouldn't care to know about."

He half-smiled and dropped the subject, understanding enough. Then taking the TV remote, he started flipping the stations.

"Where's this roommate of yours?"

"I don't know," I answered, glancing over to him from underneath my hair, admiring him as he nonchalantly switched the channels. "Are you wondering if she's cute?"

He quickly looked in my direction. "Wha... what?! No!" he defended.

Giggling and removing the remote from his hand, I said, "She's at her boyfriend's apartment tonight. She texted to say she won't be here."

"Oh," he nodded, raising his eyebrows happily.

"Should we go to the bedroom?" I asked.

"No need," he replied, as he brushed my hair away from jawline and began his trail of kisses there.

The next morning, I looked out my bedroom window to see that a decent amount of snow had fallen, and I figured we needed to pay a visit to see Luke before the weather got any worse. I also needed to check in on my own patients before they considered me MIA.

"Michael," I said with a gentle shove to his shoulder. Being persistent, I tried again, but with only a muffled grunt as a response from him, I decided to let him sleep and got up to get ready.

After a shower and quickly dressing, then starting a pot of coffee, I peeked back in to see that he was still sawing logs. Unsure of whether to let him sleep or wake him, I let time be the deciding factor and poured myself a cup of coffee, sitting down on the stool at the breakfast table.

"Good morning," Jennie, my roommate, said as she walked in the door. "What's new with you?" she asked.

Not wanting to tell her about Michael yet, I replied, "Nothing much. Just getting ready to head to the hospital for the day."

Glancing around the room, she quickly noticed Michael's boots and jacket.

"No!" I panicked inside my head.

"Mmmhm, which is why I see a man's boots and jacket laying over there. What's the scoop?" she asked, pouring some coffee, sitting down across from me.

"No scoop..."

"You're the roommate?" he asked, walking into the room in only his boxers, hair messy, motioning for some coffee.

"I'm Jennie. You are?" she asked, eyebrows raised, obviously checking him out.

"I'm Michael."

He sat down on the barstool next to me, took a drink of my coffee while I was getting his cup, and he started the questioning.

I could tell Jennie wasn't at all what Michael was expecting because he looked her way several times with a quizzical brow, and I think he'd never imagined that I'd had a petite, lively, Asian chef for a roommate. I'm sure he was expecting a voluptuous blonde, or a tell-it-like-it-is girl similar to me, to help me run my life. But he never expected what he actually walked in on— Jennie Hirano— award-winning Japanese chef.

"So, Jennie, Hadley says you're a chef."

"Yes. What do you do, Michael?"

"Nothing good."

"Okay, so you're a jokester. I mean, what's your job?"

I handed him his coffee and answered for him, knowing Jennie wasn't going to get any answers talking directly to him.

"He's a real estate attorney."

"Only on days that end in Y."

"Wait... what?" she asked.

He laughed, picked up his mug, kissed my cheek, and whispered, "I'm going to go take a shower." Then he walked away with his mug to the bathroom.

"He's..."

"He's fantastic," I said, watching him walk away.

"You really like this guy?" Jennie asked.

"Yeah, I do."

"I've got to hand it to you, Had. He's... Mmm! Where did you find this guy?"

"He was working as my parents' farmhand. We just clicked right away and it became more than sex, I guess."

"What's he doing in the city then?" she asked, pouring herself a cup of coffee.

"It's so sad. His best friend was in a motorcycle accident and is seriously injured. I transferred him here..."

"And now you're going to play doctor. I know you, Hady. You can't do this."

Collapsing my head onto the bar in front of me, I said, "I know."

"Do you love this guy?" she asked, walking toward the hallway to head to her room.

"Maybe."

"Then you shouldn't be working so closely with what he loves," she said.

"Why not?" I hollered after her.

"Because you love it too."

Eleven

"How is he?" I asked Luke's attending as I entered and glanced through the chart.

"Not really much happening as far as changes. I saw some spiking on his EEG this morning, which showed me he was having some possible seizure activity in his frontal lobe."

"Which means he is having more activity..." I said enthusiastically, before being interrupted.

"Yes, but seizure activity is not a good thing. We need to see steady, calm waves."

I nodded and walked out, asking the nurse to keep me informed of any progress being made.

Weeks went by and his situation didn't seem to be looking any better. After two brain surgeries to repair bleeds and a shunt insertion, I was beginning to fear the worst.

"What are you doing?" Michael asked as I pulled the drop-down ladder out of the door in the ceiling.

"It's time."

"What's time?" he asked.

Instead of answering, I climbed up the ladder and crawled in through the square hole in the ceiling.

When he hollered up to me again, I leaned my head back out and answered, "It's time for Christmas!" Then I disappeared into the attic crawl-space once again.

A few minutes later, I heard movement on the ladder, and then I heard his voice directly behind me.

"How can I help?"

"Oh!" I exclaimed, turning to look back at him from where I was crouched down on my hands and knees, sorting boxes. I shoved a large tree box over to him.

"You take that one. It's heavy."

He nodded, heaving over his shoulder, descending the ladder.

"Be careful!" I hollered down to him.

As soon as I got down, with my boxes in hand, I looked over to the empty space near the window, which was actually no longer empty because he had already taken out the tree and assembled it.

Happy at the sight, I smiled and dropped my boxes onto the coffee table, walking up from behind him, wrapping my arms around him tightly.

"Thanks," I said. "That usually takes me forever, plus a stool."

"Well, it's my pleasure. What's in the boxes?"

"The ornaments. Let's get to decorating."

I turned on the Christmas music as we put on the ornaments and I was certain I heard a quiet humming from him when Santa Claus is Comin' to Town came on. But I wasn't certain. He willingly put up the star on top of the tree for me and laughed at my attempt to string the lights at the tip top.

"Let me get that for you," he said, taking the strands of lights from me, hanging them.

"I usually get them eventually," I replied, sticking out my tongue like a rotten kid.

"I like to help. Now. Grab those bulbs and start putting them on. Be helpful."

Continuing my sassiness, I rolled my eyes and hung a bulb.

Once we were finished, we plopped down onto the couch and snuggled up together watching the snow fall outside.

"Time for hot chocolate?" I asked.

"Okay," he replied, standing to go to the kitchen. "Marshmallows?"

Watching him walk away and enjoying the image, I replied, "Yeah."

When he handed me my mug, he said, "Thanks for doing all of this with me."

"What?"

"Regular things."

Curious about his comment, I said, "Why don't you keep in touch with your family?"

"I had a rough time when my mom passed."

"Where's your dad?"

"I don't know."

After saying that, he placed his mug on the coffee table and walked down the hallway to my room, not returning for several minutes.

My thoughts turned to his family and how it must've been very difficult for him to lose his mother and I wondered what was the cause of her death.

"Medical, possibly? She couldn't have been very old. Cancer is likely. Perhaps that's why he said he was smiling at the irony..." I thought but was interrupted.

"Merry Christmas Eve, Hadley," Michael said, handing me a small box.

"A present?" I beamed.

"Just open it." He handed it to me but with a look of reservation.

"Okay. I'm so excited!" I tore into the beautifully wrapped package to see a jewelry box, and I couldn't help the small gasp that escaped from my mouth at the sight. "Michael?"

"Just open it," he said once more.

Inside the little black jewelry box was a delicate rose gold heart-shaped locket.

"It's gorgeous!" I exclaimed.

"Open it."

I clicked it open and saw that he'd put our faces inside. My heart filled with too many emotions to even describe and I just sat, staring at the most beautiful, thoughtful Christmas present I'd ever received.

"Eventually I'm going to have to return to Colorado and you'll stay here. I don't want you to forget about the beautiful time we spent together, not ever, no matter what happens to me in the future."

"What do you mean?'

"I just mean that we can't ever predict what life has in store."

Turning to face him, I studied his face carefully and decided that he was saying more than he was trying to show, but I didn't want to ruin the moment. So, I held the locket out for him to clasp around my neck, and I said, "I could never forget you. You were my way home. Besides, it's the most beautiful present I've ever received. Thank you."

"You are my way home too."

"What do you mean?"

He didn't answer me, only kissed my forehead and got up, washed his mug, and walked to the shower.

"Jennie," I said a few evenings later, walking into the apartment. "What do you feel like making for eats?"

"Where have you been?! I've been calling you for hours!" she yelled despair and sadness all over her face.

"Um, work. I'm a doctor. I work a lot," I replied.

I would've reacted more to my petite roommate's hysteria; however, she had the tendency to get anxious and nervous about everything. So, I asked, "What's going on?"

"I tried to call you a thousand times. When you didn't answer your cell, I wasn't sure what else to do." She shrugged and pointed to the bloody towels balled up near the washer in the corner.

"Where's Michael?'

"I'm not sure."

"Seeing Luke?"

"He got sick and then he left in a hurry. I'll call for a ride."

I walked into the ER at Regions and immediately I looked for the attending physician in order to find out exactly what was going on.

"Dr. Todd?" I said, entering the back of the ER.

"Dr. Crashaw, what are you doing down here? How can I be of assistance?"

"It's possible you have my boyfriend as one of your patients."

"I can certainly look into that. What's his name?" he asked, looking through the names on his computer.

"Michael Radcliff," I replied.

"There's no Michael Radcliff listed as a patient in my registry. It's possible he was admitted. Let me check the hospital registry."

Nervously pacing back and forth in front of the desk, I went over dozens of illnesses in my mind that would cause bloody vomit, but it was impossible to pinpoint what was causing him to become ill so quickly, especially without knowing his medical history.

"There's no Michael Radcliff listed anywhere in the hospital registry at all. Are you sure he was admitted here?"

I hurried away and back out of the hospital before he could even finish, dialing Michael's cell.

"Michael," I said to his voicemail, "It's Hadley. Jennie told me you got sick. Please call me back. I'm very worried."

Unsure of what to do next, I dialed my mother.

"Mama?"

"Hi, sweetie. Why are you crying?"

My whole heart collapsed and I didn't know what to say, think, or do, so I hung up. Standing outside the ER entrance to my hospital, I felt helpless. Without even a thought of what I should do with myself, I just started walking. I didn't know how else to react to the situation, so I walked. Apparently, it was the right thing to do because I came across a "bum" looking for a ride inside a bar.

"Just get out of here!" the bartender yelled.

"I'm only looking for a way home!" Michael yelled back.

"Michael! Are you drunk?" I yelled, hurrying up behind him.

"No," he replied almost mockingly.

"Yes, you are!"

"Hadley, don't push this. Just walk away."

"I will not! I am getting you somewhere safe. Let's go!" I yelled, pulling on his arm.

But he knocked me back and onto the ground, yelling, "Forget it! Walk away!"

Afraid at what he was becoming in his drunken state, I let him walk off and I returned to the hospital and sat in my office arms crossed on my desk head face down in my arms, feeling despair.

However, I didn't sit that way too long before I was alerted on the hospital PA.

DR. CRASHAW TO E.R. THREE. DR. CRASHAW TO E.R. THREE.

My head jumped up off my desk faster than humanly possible, or so it felt.

"Michael!" I thought, as my legs carried me through the halls and to the elevator to the basement floor where the ER was held until I walked into room three.

"Dr. Crashaw," one of the head E.R. nurses said to me as I walked in.

"What is it?" I asked.

"He asked for you specifically, though the doctors believe it to be liver failure..." she began as I walked away and saw Michael lying there.

It was obviously liver failure and I should've known it from the first sign— the reaction he had when I fell onto him in the hay field. He had pain in his right side— his liver.

Now the more progressive signs I saw as he was lying there on the hospital bed which showed me that this didn't sneak up on him overnight— he knew. I should've known. He was always drinking some kind of alcoholic beverage. He brought this upon himself. There's no way he didn't know and the episode with the bloody vomit couldn't have been the first. His abdomen was swollen and his skin was beginning to jaundice. How did I not see it before now?

"Michael?" I said, walking over. "You asked for me?"

He looked up, took my hand, and said, "I'm sorry about what I said. It wasn't me. I have a long history of a Michael that you wouldn't like."

"It's okay. My patients can often get a little mouthy."

He smiled and kissed my hand, then he said, "I need you to fix me."

Twelve

When I left Hadley's apartment after vomiting up so much blood, I knew I needed to get as far away from her as possible. As much as I loved Hadley, I couldn't let her become any more attached and ruin her life.

"I'm going to call for an ambulance," Jennie said.

"I'm alright," I replied, walking to the door, pulling out my cell phone.

"Michael! Hadley is at the hospital! Go to Regions and ask for her!" she hollered behind as I slammed the door closed.

"The airport," I said to the cabbie when he pulled up and I got in.

"Midway?" he asked.

"O'Hare," I said.

"You got it."

However, just as he began driving down the street, the worst happened.

"Buddy? You okay back there? I'm taking you to the hospital!" he yelled as I vomited blood all over his back seat.

He pulled up outside of Regions ER and said, "It's on me, man. Hope you're okay. ER is right there." Then he pulled away. But as I stood looking at the ER knowing that Hadley would surely find out everything that I'd been hiding, I couldn't go inside. Three blocks away I had noticed a bar—I went there instead.

"Bourbon," I said to the bartender.

"Are you sure buddy? You don't look so good," he replied.

"I'm sure."

He reached for the bourbon and began pouring me shot after shot, but when I started asking other customers for rides to the airport, he questioned what I was doing in there.

"Where are you from?" he asked.

"Colorado. I need a way to get to the airport."

"Why don't you just call a cab and stop bothering my customers?" he said.

"I had a cab, but that didn't work out."

"This isn't going to work out either, pal. Why don't you pay for your shots and get out of here?"

"Look," I said, in a very drunken state. "I just need a way home."

"You aren't getting that in here. Pay for your shots and get out. Leave the other customers alone."

When he said that, I vomited blood all over the bar floor. Infuriated, he grabbed me up by my shirt collar and tossed me outside.

"Just get out of here!" he yelled.

"I'm only looking for a way home," I replied.

But that's when I saw her. Hadley was there. Like an angel, she came to my rescue. But did I let her? No.

"Michael? Are you drunk?" she asked.

"No," I said almost laughing. I was drunker than a skunk and could hardly stand up at that point, but I wasn't admitting it to her.

"Yes, you are!" she yelled.

"Hadley, don't push this. Just walk away," I said, wanting her to leave me alone, desperately just wanting to find a ride to the airport, but also knowing she was never going to drop this. "Hadley, don't push this. Just walk away."

"I will not! I am getting you somewhere safe. Let's go!" she yelled, pulling on my arm.

However, my drunken anger took over in me, causing me to toss her back and onto the ground, yelling, "Forget it! Walk away!"

When I saw the fear and hurt in her eyes, I was immediately regretful for my actions, and I feared I would never earn her forgiveness. I told Luke from the first day I met her that she was too good for me and I'd meant it. She was too good for me. Now I was watching her walk away. A few moments after, I followed. I needed to fix this and I would start by letting her fix me.

"May I help you?" the ER triage nurse asked.

"I need to be seen," I said, sitting down.

"Symptoms?" she asked.

"I know exactly what I have and I know the doctor I want."

"Excuse me?" she said glancing up to me from the computer.

"I've been sick for a long time. I know all my symptoms. I know my diagnosis. I know the doctor I want."

"Then why are you at the ER?"

"Because I'm vomiting blood."

Not too long after, I was being taken into a room and dressed in a gown, and I heard them page for her over the hospital P.A.

However, I wasn't sure how she would feel about seeing me after I'd treated her so terribly.

"Michael?" she said, walking into my room a little while later.

Thinking I should start with an apology, I said, "I'm sorry about what I said. It wasn't me. I have a long history of a Michael that you wouldn't like..."

"It's okay. My patients can often get a little mouthy," she replied, and right then I knew without the shadow of a doubt that I loved this beautiful, intelligent, angel of a doctor.

I smiled and kissed her hand, and thinking on her words for a moment I said, "I need you to fix me."

"I see that you probably have a pretty advanced stage liver disease."

"Hadley, I have liver cancer."

Her face turned to shock, then sadness as she soaked in the reality of what I'd just said to her.

Standing to pace the room, hand to her forehead to think, she began asking questions.

"What is it?"

"Hepatocellular Carcinoma," I said, and immediately she had a look of relief.

"You just need a transplant. This is good news! I'll put you on the donor list immediately." She walked over and kissed my cheek, then walked out.

"I need to add a patient to the donor registry," I said to my boss, walking into his office

"The patient needs to be approved by the board and needs to pass all the..."

Tears filled my eyes and emotions flooded my heart. "No!" I called out. "We don't have time for all of that. He is dying. If he doesn't get on this list, he is going to lose his life." I began sobbing so vehemently that my boss stood and walked over to me, leading me to a chair.

"Dr. Hadley, is this a patient who is a relative of yours?"

I sniffled a few times and then said, "He is my boyfriend. He has a rare blood type. He needs a liver transplant for a Hepatocellular Carcinoma. Please let me add him."

"I wish there was something I could do Hadley, but my hands are tied. Go through the process and..."

Knowing that sentence was leading exactly to Michael's death, I walked out and refused to accept there was nothing they could do and decided to come up with a plan of my own. He would never be approved for the donor wait list with his reason for liver cancer—alcoholism—and even if he did, he would wait forever for a donor because of his rare blood type.

In order to think for a while, I decided to check on his friend and hopefully give Michael some good news.

I walked into Luke's room without much confidence that anything would be looking any better, but I hoped...for Michael.

"How is he today, Missy?" I asked the nurse as she changed his drip. "Actually..."

If hearts could've stopped just from seeing someone's eyes awake and alert, then my heart would have been frozen in my chest right then and there. "Luke?" I said, hurrying over to him. "How are you? No one alerted me that you were awake."

When he didn't turn his head to me, I understood right away that he had very limited mobility and I immediately logged into his computer and quickly looked over his chart, but the words I read crushed me.

"I'm looking at your chart right now," I said to him as I watched the ventilator manually pump his chest up and down.

I read through the chart before then I said, "You're choosing to end your life support..."

As a girlfriend, I wanted to talk Luke out of his decision. Hadley Crashaw loved Michael Radcliff, and I knew Luke was Michael's best friend. Losing him was going to crush Michael, whatever the reason. But as a professional, Dr. Crashaw needed to honor the request, whatever the reason.

"I need to let Michael know your decision. He won't be able to come and see you, however," I said, approaching the bedside, grasping his hand. "Michael is very ill. His liver is failing him..."

Luke let out a few grunts and I knew that he was trying to communicate something with me, so I got a piece of paper for him to write. After he scribbled a few sentences I read it out loud.

"I know about Michael. He's been sick for a while. When I terminate life support, my liver is to go to him. It's all written in my paperwork; my doctors know, but I'm assuming you're his doctor and you should know."

Unsure of how to respond to that and feeling shocked and actually a little grieved since Michael was about to lose his best friend, I only put the paper aside and walked out to speak to his doctors.

"Luke has requested termination of his life support?"

"He has a clause in his living will that says if he were to ever be on prolonged life support that it should be terminated. But this is good news for your boyfriend," his doctor said.

"How so?!" I exclaimed, tossing my hands up, tears filling my eyes. "Luke is his best friend."

"Well, your boyfriend needs a liver and has a rare blood type. Luke wrote that upon his death, he is donating his liver to Michael. With his

AB- blood, it's a perfect match. It's almost like Luke knew Mike was going to need it and timed it perfectly. Weird, isn't it?"

"It is weird," I sighed.

Soon after, there was a discussion in his room with the doctors and nurses, and I watched from the hallway as he signed the papers and scheduled the day. Tears rolled slowly from my eyes knowing it was inevitable and that Michael wouldn't even get to say goodbye, but I tried remembering that Luke was doing it for him.

Tears dripping, heart breaking, I walked the long corridor to head down to Michael's room.

He was awake when I entered and wondered why I was so sad, and I had no idea how on earth I was ever going to tell him that his best friend was discontinuing life support. But not only was Luke discontinuing life support, but Luke was also doing it and using it as a means to save his life.

"You've been crying," Michael said. "What's the matter?"

"I have a patient who is choosing to end his treatment option."

"I'm so sorry. It must be hard for you to lose patients." He took my hand, kissed it, and scooted to make room for me on the bed.

"It is. But it will be even harder when it's one I love. We need to make you well."

I leaned down to kiss his forehead and he said, "Have you been in to see Luke?"

Hesitant to tell him any details of Luke's decision, I only said, "Yes. I saw him a little while ago."

"How is he today? Any change?" he asked.

Unable to lie but also unable to shatter his hopes, I merely replied, "There was much change today."

As I watched a little excitement cross his face, I felt bad for doing that to him, so I retracted a bit and asked, "Does he have any family? Any at all?"

"I don't like the way this is going, Hadley."

Standing to pace the floor beside the bed, unable to tell the only man I'd ever loved that his best friend was about to give up his life to donate his liver for him, I took his hand, kissed his knuckles and said, "I have some patients I need to see. I'll be back in a little while. Why don't you get some rest? Don't order dinner. I'll bring you the doctor's special." I winked, blew him a kiss, then walked out and went directly for the phone.

"Dr. Erickson? It's Dr. Crashaw. I don't need to put my patient on the list now. We are scheduling him for surgery first thing tomorrow."

Thirteen

"Michael?" the nurse said as she coached me, trying to get me to wake in recovery. "Wake up dear. How do you feel?"

"I'm okay. Can Dr. Hadley come to see me?" I asked.

"She was just in here, dear. She will return shortly. She wanted to be paged when you woke. She needed to see her other patients." Then she checked my incision and added, "You know, I think you're more than a patient to her. You should take advantage of the fancy that doctor has taken to you. She's very pretty."

Smiling slightly, I said, "She is and I will. Thanks."

A little while later, Hadley returned to check in on me.

"How's my favorite patient?" she asked, kissing my cheek, only after making sure no one was looking.

"I'm fine. I'm only wondering about Luke."

The look on her face told me that all was not well, and the next sentence she said changed everything.

"Remember when I told you I had a patient who was choosing to end his treatment option?"

"Yes."

"Well, as a doctor, I have to honor that request…"

"What are you saying?"

Hesitant to reply, she stood and hid her face in her hands and I could tell she was crying, so I tried assuring her that it was going to be fine.

"Hadley, it's going to be fine. How is Luke?"

She looked over to me, tears flooding her eyes, and she said, "Luke chose to end his life support this morning. You have his liver."

"Go."

"Michael... I..."

"Your job as a doctor is to fix people. You did the exact opposite to him. You broke him! You failed him. I want you gone! I never want to see you again! I am requesting a new doctor."

She didn't cry or speak; she didn't look at me; she walked out and never looked back. Watching her go, I immediately realized the harshness of my words and regretted my behavior and couldn't believe myself for the way I'd behaved to her.

When I asked the nurse to page for her, the nurse only told me that Dr. Hadley was unavailable and I feared that she was avoiding me.

Later that day, a new doctor came in to see me— Dr. King.

"Let's take a look here and see how you're doing, shall we?" he said.

"Who are you?" I asked.

"I'm your new attending," he answered as he checked my chart and looked over my incision.

"Where's Dr. Crashaw?" I asked.

"Dr. Hadley is no longer with us."

"What do you mean?"

"She resigned her position earlier today."

THREE WEEKS LATER

"It's nice to have you back, Mr. Radcliff," Gayle said as I walked in and took the mail from her, but I didn't respond as I wasn't in a chatty mood. However, Gayle was relentless.

"Where's our pretty doctor? Not hanging around anymore, I see. Do we need an apology present? I will send one straight away. Mr. Crashaw called this morning and mentioned that the mattress you ordered for him was delivered and he greatly appreciates it and invited you out for supper. Said to have you call if you're interested. Also, this letter was mailed here with no return address..."

"Perfect!" I exclaimed. It was exactly as I had been waiting for but had been interrupted because of all the chaos that erupted. I hoped it was enough to win Hadley's heart again, but I feared it never would.

"Mr. Crashaw? It's Michael. Meet me at my office as soon as you can."

After speaking with Mr. Crashaw and fixing what had needed to be fixed from the moment I met Hadley, I went to the big blue house and took care of one last issue.

Then I sat and wrote her a long letter and mailed it to her at the farm because I knew that's where she'd be. Once all that was done, I gave up.

MICHAEL'S WORDS AT the hospital crushed me, my spirit, and my will to continue practicing medicine. I tried so hard for him and Luke, but it hadn't been good enough. Doctors aren't God. We are only human. We fail too. When I walked out of his room, I vowed I would never look in his way again, nor would I ever practice medicine again.

"Dr. Hadley?" a nurse said to me on my way down the hall.

"Ask someone else. I resign."

When I got back to my office to pack up my things, my boss met me in there to figure out what he could do to get me to stay.

"We all lose patients, Hadley. What is it you need?"

"I just need a way home."

Once I returned to the farm, I spent two days crying on my bed and I never left my room. My mother offered me numerous times to get me something to eat but I refused. I even heard my father talk about Michael, which only made it all the worse.

"I'm meeting Michael in town. Do you ladies need anything? What about you, Hady?"

But I said no. I wanted Michael out of my life and head. I was heartbroken.

Soon after, though, he returned absolutely ecstatic babbling something about the sale of the farm and handing me a letter.

Hadley,

No words I could ever say to you would ever be enough to earn your forgiveness, which is why I have to show you how sorry I am. Even if I never accomplish that goal, I have to try. You're the only woman I've ever loved and you're the greatest doctor I've ever had. You need to know it. I bought the farm and now I'm giving it back to you with the freedom to sell it. Attached to this letter it the free deed, paid for, owned by you, (will be once you come to the blue house and sign your name), and no longer with the stipulation to sell it in as a whole. I love you, Hadley. I would do anything for you.

Love,

Michael

WHEN I ARRIVED AT THE blue house, the sight before me was enough to stop my heart or make it beat again, whichever was the case that needed to be.

The sign outside read:

Dr. Hadley Crashaw M.D.

I knew Michael was extraordinary, but how extraordinary he was, I hadn't yet experienced. I walked inside, but he wasn't there.

"Hello, Miss," his secretary said.

"Oh," I said, surprised at the sight. "Where's Michael?" I asked.

"He believed you wouldn't want him here."

A few tears dripped from my eyes before I said, "Well that's just obviously not true," and then I walked inside and the beautiful image I saw made me fall in love with him even more, and whatever problems we were experiencing felt like they no longer existed.

"Gayle? Where is he?" I asked.

"I'm not sure. I haven't seen him in days."

"When did he do all of this?" I asked, walking around, looking at the personalized doctor's office he had set up for me with a waiting room, my own office, patient rooms, and a picture of Luke.

"He put it into motion a few weeks ago, said something about messing it up big-time with you..."

As she said those words, I hurried out the front door and to the bar a few doors down.

My thoughts drifted to everything that went wrong and how quickly it turned so badly for everyone. "Where did I screw it all up?" I wondered, wiping my tears. "It wouldn't have worked anyway. We are too different."

"Anyone here know Michael Radcliff?" I asked when I walked in, wanting to get down to business.

"Are you Hadley Crashaw?" the bartender asked me.

"Yes," I said, walking closer.

"Mikey frequents here. Well, until recently. What you need to know? Have a seat... on the house," she said getting out a glass.

"Just a water, please. That stuff will kill you," I said. But when I said that, she frowned and looked to the man sitting next to me.

"I take it that's why you're here?" the man next to me asked.

"What?"

"About Mikey," he continued,

"I returned to Chicago a few weeks ago. I just came back today."

"Hell, you better come on then." He snatched me up by my arm and dragged me outside, practically tossing me onto his motorcycle.

"Put this on," he said, handing me a helmet, "And hold on tight. It's a long ride."

"Where are we going?"

"To Pierce Memorial."

"Pierce Memorial?" I thought. "The hospital?"

He sped through those back roads so fast that I couldn't even look up and I didn't care at all that he was some scruffy bar man. I buried my face in his back and clung to him all the more.

When we arrived, I waited for direction, but he just took my hand and we got visitor passes and went to the fourth floor...

ICU

"No!" I thought.

Rm. 451

The rough biker man knocked and walked in before me. Hesitantly, I followed.

"Mikey!" he said. "I brought you a gift. I hope it's okay. I'm going to wait downstairs though. I'll be back in a little while. I hope you're doing okay today, pal." Then he turned around and waved for me to come inside.

"Hadley?" he said.

"Michael?" I responded, wiping tears from my eyes. "What are you doing here? What's going on?" I asked.

"It's just time."

"What?!"

"How could you let it all come to this?!" I yelled, tears dripping from my cheeks.

"Hadley, I had no idea..."

I stormed out of there wanting answers, searching for his doctors.

"Excuse me, nurse."

"Yes?" she replied.

"I'm a friend of Mr. Radcliff, but I'm also an oncology fellow at Regions. I have ID. I would like to see his chart."

"Certainly, once he authorizes that for us," she said.

"Excuse me?"

"He has to authorize you as an approved medical provider."

She walked away.

Furious, I went back into his room, but I calmly explained what I wanted him to do.

"I want you to add me as a medical provider."

He looked over to me with a confused expression, so I repeated myself.

"I tried to look at your medical file, but they won't allow me to see it until you authorize me as an approved medical provider.

"Okay."

Happiness crossed my face and I felt like there could be some hope until he said, "Why? Are you just being nosy? Because then my answer is no."

"Oh. Um... I want to help. This is what I do."

"Okay then."

"Perfect. I'll tell the nurse."

"Hadley?" he said, reaching his arm out.

Walking back over to him, I sat on the edge of the hospital bed and held his hand.

"Yeah?"

"Thank you for coming back."

I sighed satisfactorily and laid down beside him, then I whispered, "I need to be here. I realized I love you too."

"I know."

"What?" I said, sitting up, looking at his once bright blue eyes that were now looking a pale gray color.

"I know you do, which is why you want to be sure I'm getting the best care. But that is why I can't let you be my doctor."

"Why not? I'm an amazing doctor!" I protested.

"I know you are. And I want you to keep believing that about yourself. But I know who I am and who I can be. I also know the reality of my situation and the gravity of it. If you are my doctor instead of the woman who loves me, you'll never look at yourself the same way again. When I die, your belief in yourself and your abilities will change even though it wouldn't be your fault just like it wasn't with Luke. I'm sorry about how I reacted with Luke. I was grieving..."

"I know..."

"Hadley, just be here with me."

"You're not going to die. We are going to fix you. Fixing people is what I do!"

He only nodded, and I figured he was feeling fatigued, which would've been assumed given his current situation— he was rejecting his transplant. I wanted him to rest, so I helped him get into a more comfortable position and I sat down next to him. But then he asked me the question I was hoping he would.

"You went to the blue house? You got my letter?"

I nodded and didn't ask anything else, but it concerned me that he didn't mention the woman who'd used to live there. Even in all the madness and chaos that was happening in my family, I would still want to know if one of my brothers was dying. Maybe we were fortunate in that sense, but I was worried that she would want to see him.

As he fell back asleep, I brushed the hair away from his face and stood to go look for a doctor in order to get some more information about his condition. Even if I couldn't have complete access to his file, I still wanted to know the basics of what was happening with him.

I wandered the hall looking for a white coat until I found someone I thought might be an attending physician.

"Excuse me..." I extended my hand and shook his hand while I looked for the name tag. "Dr. Morris?"

"Yes?" he asked.

Knowing I couldn't get any information unless I was intimately involved with Michael, I said, "I'm the girlfriend of Michael..."

"Mr. Radcliff?" he finished.

"Yes."

"I'm not his primary physician, but I can fill you in on some details."

"I should let you know that I'd like to know it from a fellow physician's perspective," I said, showing him my hospital ID.

"I would be glad to do that. Why don't we chat in my office?" He nodded and pointed to a side hallway.

My heart was filled with despair as I walked in and saw him pull Michael's chart up on a tablet, scrolling through a few screens as we sat down across from each other at his desk.

Even more so than the despair, my heart was feeling at that moment was the worry that had crept over my mind at the thought that I couldn't fix this.

"Michael came to us because the recent transplant is believed to be failing…" Dr. Morris began, and after a long explanation about his options and what they believed Michael should do, I interrupted and said, "What treatment has he received?"

"He was counseled on all his options, but Michael is here because he discontinued his medication on his own. He has no will to live."

Before he could finish, I stood and walked out of the office and raced back to the room to see Michael's nurse changing his pain meds.

"Could you give us a minute please?" I asked and walked over to him as he sat up to look at me.

"Are you okay?" he asked me, puzzled.

"You refused all treatment options?"

He didn't answer, only looking away, somewhat shamed.

"Why?! How could you do that?" I yelled.

"Hadley…"

I interrupted, "I'm so angry!"

"Please don't be angry. I got sick two years ago." He looked back to me as I sat in the chair next to his bed, and then he said, "I didn't plan on you."

"What?" I looked up.

"Janine, my sister, threw me out when I was a recovering drunk and she was all I had. She didn't know that the liver cirrhosis turned into a tumor. I used some money I had to buy the house I live in now and I've been living there. But that blue house is mine. She only lives there."

"But that was two years ago. Why didn't you take the medicine now?"

"I don't have a reason to live."

"Isn't life enough of a reason?" I asked, taking his hand.

"Hadley, I was a recovering drunk with liver cancer. What did I have to live for?"

"Me."

"I'm sorry."

"Take the treatments. Let me see your chart."

"I can't let you be my doctor," he said, motioning for me sit beside him.

"But I want to fix you," I said, leaning up to kiss his cheek.

"But you already have."

Michael Radcliff was the love of my life, yet he never took any treatments to help his liver transplant or liver cancer. He left the hospital on January 29. He died Christmas Day the following year inside the big blue house in the room with the circular window.

"Promise me something," he said as I brought tea that morning.

"Anything."

"Keep this house."

"You want me to have it?" I asked.

"I don't care if you don't keep using it as a doctor's office, but please don't get rid of it. You're the most important person in the whole world to me and knowing that this house has you in it makes me die a happy man."

I smiled and knelt down next to the bed he was lying in and said, "*That's* what's made you a happy man?"

He chuckled slightly and replied, "Well..."

Planting a soft kiss on his lips I said, "It's hard not to be angry at you."

"I know."

"The doctor inside of me wants to fix this and make it all better."

"Hadley, look at me." He took my face in his hands and pulled it to look him in the eyes. When I looked at his tired, darkened eyes, I just wanted to help him and see the once bright blue eyes I had seen when we first met. Placing my hands over his where they were holding my face, I said, "I'm looking."

"The last thing I was expecting when you stepped off that train that day was *you*. But when I turned down those treatments, I started praying for answers to life's toughest questions because I had to. Never before had I prayed or sought out a higher power. I didn't think I needed to. But I prayed for an angel and I was sent you. I didn't pray for a miracle because I didn't really want that. I just wanted to make my last days on this earth livable and you did that. You made life worth living. Thank you. You're all I've ever needed."

I moved his hand to my lips, kissing it softly before saying, "Now you're my downfall, Michael Radcliff."

Only a few seconds later, he breathed his last and my heart was crushed at the sound.

"I will never forget you. How could I? I loved you first."

A YEAR LATER.

"Put his picture in that room there," I said, pointing to the corner room with the circle window.

"Dr. Hadley, where should we put the memorial plaque?" one of the workers asked.

"Above the fireplace, thank you."

As I continued to give instructions, I walked out and looked around at all that was going on inside the old, blue house and was pleased with the sight and I just stood to watch as people hustled by to put the finishing touches on everything for the opening day.

"This is a good thing you're doing here," Janine said to me as she walked up. "I'm sorry for everything that happened with us and I'm even more sorry that he never told me and I wasn't there for him." She wiped her tears before she continued. "When I found out what you were doing here and read about Michael's story in the local paper, it broke my heart that he..." She shook her head and discontinued speaking.

"I know. It was hard on me too. That's why I felt it necessary to keep his memory alive."

"I feel like the worst sister in the whole world for throwing him out the way I did. I just wish I could reverse time," she sniffled and wiped more tears.

"Come with me," I said, taking her hand and leading her out to the front walkway. Once outside, I pointed to the signage that was just put up.

"Oh, Dr. Hadley... it brings tears to my eyes."

"He deserves it."

The Radcliff Foundation

Where Everyone Deserves Life

... read the sign on the front of the old blue house.

"In honor of his struggles, now no one will ever have to wonder if they have a reason to live."

"It's so beautiful. I wish he could see it," she said as her tears came harder now. "I also wish that he had you longer."

"I wish that too, but I think I came at just the right time."

After the festivities, I returned to an empty farm since my parents had already moved out and I was just counting the days until someone bought that old house from me.

But that evening in particular, I was feeling especially lonely, and I decided to walk out past the field where the old barns used to sit before they were torn down for development.

Knowing that the hunter's shed would still be there, I walked into the woods and parted the trees. A smile crossed my face when I saw it there and I climbed up. Even more, happiness overwhelmed me when I saw that Michael's things were still in there— the flashlights, battery lantern, and blankets— and I quickly took a seat, getting cozy.

"Michael," I whispered, "Show me that everything is going to be okay." I laid down, wrapped up in the blanket and let tears saturate my eyes as I thought about all the time I'd spent with Michael, and I became angry at myself for not recognizing the signs of his illness.

"You should've known," I whispered. "You're a doctor. You should've seen the signs."

After crying a few minutes, I wiped my eyes and turned on the battery with the intention of looking out to see the deer. But a message written on the wall stopped my intentions.

Hadley,

I left these things for you. Please get great use of them. You might have been my downfall, but you weren't a mistake. I love you.

Michael

"Michael," I whispered, "I deal with death every day, but I never thought it would ever be as difficult as this."

I laid there wrapped in his blankets for hours until my body was too cold to stay in there any longer and I finally surrendered.

"Good night, Michael."

The next day, I drove to the old blue house unprepared for what was ahead of me as I opened the door and walked inside.

"Good morning, Dr. Hadley. There is a patient here to see you. We sent him to the corner room."

"Where is his file?" I asked.

"On your desk," Gayle said as I walked away and to my office.

Picking the file up off of my desk, I was taken aback by the name at first sight and I dropped the file onto my desk, walking out to look at the patient's face.

"Is this some kind of sick joke?" I asked, crying.

"Dr. Hadley?" she said.

The man stood, leaning on a cane, reached out his hand, and said, "I'm Michael Radcliff Sr. I saw the sign out front and I was curious about the story. You are taking new patients?"

Looking at the man, I saw the spitting image of my Michael, 20 years his senior,s and I remembered his words *What do I have to live for?*

Yet, here I was standing in front of his own father seeing exactly how much he'd had to live for.

"Yes. I'm Dr. Hadley Crashaw. It's a pleasure to finally meet you. What can I do for you?"

"Well, I hear you're the best."

"Oh? Who recommended me?" I asked as I held my stethoscope to his chest.

"My son."

His words startled me because I hadn't realized they'd spoken about me so I asked, "Your son, Michael?"

He turned to face me and said, "He told me that I shouldn't make the same mistake he made with his life."

"What was that?" I asked.

"I should live."

At that moment, I knew that Michael had heard my request in the hunter's shed and that he was letting me know that everything was going to be alright after all.

"Thank you," I said, and though I said it to Michael Sr., I truly meant it for my Michael.

Thanks for reading and I hope you enjoyed this novella! If you liked this, leave a review, and please check out my other book, MY LAST BREATH, a five-star rated novel. Thanks for reading! You can follow me on Twitter and Instagram @ Megswritesbooks or Facebook @ www.Facebook.com/Megsechrestwrites[1]

Visit my website for more information about upcoming novels!

---

1. http://www.facebook.com/Megsechrestwrites

Acknowledgements

As always, I want to thank my husband who is always stepping up and taking my place around the house when I hide myself behind the computer for days, weeks, and months at a time to write these books. Kevin, I can never thank you enough for your support.

Lola, thank you for this beautiful book cover and always being there to make an image, draft a cover, listen to me complain, and to do pretty much anything I want. We are both underpaid. But neither would change it.

Carrie, thanks for always being my biggest fan. When no one else wants to read what I write, I can count on you. You're just what I need in a friend.

And just when I feel like giving up, Candace, you are always there to give me a little push. Thank you for never letting me quit. God put you into my life for a reason.

Just as before, I thank God for giving me the strength to do this even on my worst days. Deuteronomy 31:8, Isaiah 41:10, and Exodus 14:14. God, you pre-planned my life and I am grateful.

About the Author

Meg Sechrest resides in rural Ohio with her husband and four children. When she isn't dreaming up great stories, she likes to spend time with her family and do some sewing. Her best inspiration for writing is Jane Austen or cello music and she often takes long walks listening to classical music wondering what Jane Austen would write in a story. When people ask where she gets ideas for her books, her answer will always be, "I don't know," because she truly doesn't, and she always says that her characters will always have everything they ever wanted in life, even if they don't know that's what they wanted.

Read more at https://www.authormegsechrest.com/.